Just as he lowered his head, he heard it, stronger this time. Every muscle in his body tensed. Fainter than any human ear could possibly hear, Tam heard her voice. "Tam! Tam!"

Tam barked once, twice, then listened again. Her call came from the north. He fixed on the direction, barked again, and picked his way along the creek bank. He did not know that between him and the girl lay miles of rhododendron and mountain laurel so thick a person couldn't push through it. He could not know that it would take hours to work his way back upstream.

All he knew was she was calling. For all the years he could remember, this voice was his world, his compass. And when the person he loves most in the world calls, a dog can do nothing but go.

BOBBIE PYRON

A Dog's Way Home

KATHERINE TEGEN BOOKS

An Imprint of HarperCollins Publishers

For Teddy, Boo, and Sherlock,
my inspiration and my soul.
And for Todd,
who provided a safe home for my heart.

Katherine Tegen Books is an imprint of HarperCollins Publishers.

A Dog's Way Home
Copyright © 2011 by Bobbie Pyron
Map art copyright © 2011 by Tim Jessell

Library of Congress Cataloging-in-Publication Data
Pyron, Bobbie.
A dog's way home / Bobbie Pyron.—1st ed.
    p. cm.
    Summary: After a car accident strands them at opposite ends of the Blue
Ridge Parkway, eleven-year-old Abby and her beloved sheltie, Tam, overcome
months filled with physical and emotional challenges to find their way back
to each other.
    ISBN 978-0-06-198672-7
    [1. Shetland sheepdog—Fiction. 2. Dogs—Fiction. 3. Lost and
found possessions—Fiction. 4. Human-animal relationships—Fiction.
5. Survival—Fiction. 6. North Carolina—Fiction.] I. Title.
PZ7.P999Do 2011   2010006960
[Fic]—dc22   CIP
                                                                        AC

Typography by Andrea Vandergrift
12 13 14 15 16 LP/BR   10 9 8 7 6 5 4 3 2
❖
First paperback edition, 2012

Contents

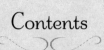

Winter

Spring

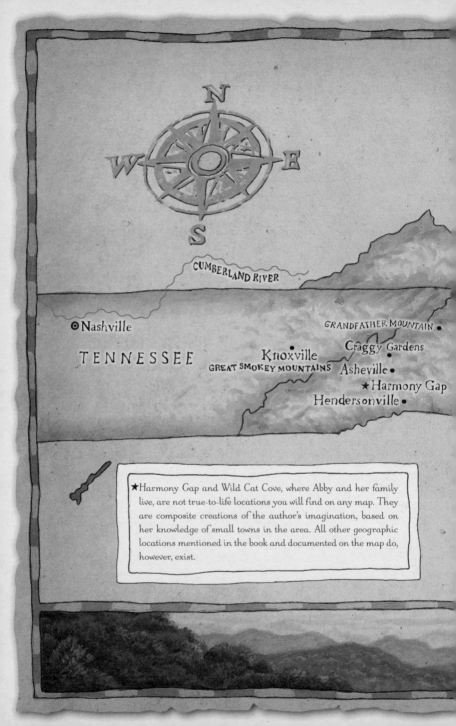

N
W   E
S

CUMBERLAND RIVER

⊙ Nashville   GRANDFATHER MOUNTAIN •

TENNESSEE   Craggy Gardens
                       Knoxville •   •
              GREAT SMOKEY MOUNTAINS   Asheville •
                                  ★ Harmony Gap
                            Hendersonville •

★Harmony Gap and Wild Cat Cove, where Abby and her family
live, are not true-to-life locations you will find on any map. They
are composite creations of the author's imagination, based on
her knowledge of small towns in the area. All other geographic
locations mentioned in the book and documented on the map do,
however, exist.

FALL

CHAPTER 1

Abby

It was a near-to-perfect fall day. The late October sky was so blue and crisp, it made my eyes hurt. And the Virginia hills, all colors with their pretty fall leaves, humped and folded around us like one of Meemaw's patchwork quilts.

Mama squeezed my shoulder. "You couldn't ask for a prettier day for a competition."

I shrugged. "Tam and I ain't here for the scenery, Mama."

Mama frowned down at me. *"Aren't*, Abby Whistler. Don't talk like a hillbilly."

Tam yipped and pawed at my leg. I bent down and scooped him up in my arms, doing my level best to ignore Mama. Tam and I weren't there for a grammar lesson, neither. We were there to win the Southeast Virginia Junior Agility Championship.

Mama reached out and tickled Tam's front paws—something I happen to know he does not like but is too polite to say.

Me and Tam watched Megan Smoot finish her run with her dog, Sydney. Sydney dodged left instead of right around the last of the three jumps and missed the final jump altogether.

"Poor Megan," Mama said. "That's going to cost her."

"That Megan has the attention span of a gnat," I said. "It ain't—isn't—Sydney's fault. He was just doing what Megan told him to do."

Megan finished and waved weakly to the audience as she disappeared into the sidelines.

The loudspeaker crackled. "Next up, ladies and gents, we have little Abby Whistler and her Shetland sheepdog, Tam. They come here all the way from Harmony Gap, North Carolina. Don't let their size and youth fool you. This is the team to beat!"

I set Tam on the grass and pulled down the bill of my lucky cap. "I don't see why everybody has to remark on my being eleven," I grumbled.

Mama laughed. "You and Tam go show them what you got."

Tam and I stepped into the arena. The agility course

2

spread out before us. We had to make it through those obstacles as fast as possible with no mistakes.

Tam sat at my left heel, looking up at me, grinning his sheltie grin. His red and white coat blazed like the dickens in the sun. The star-shaped white patch on top of his head glowed. I smiled down at him. "You ready to go tear it up, little boy?"

I watched for the signal from the judge's table. I swear, a whole flock of crows rose up from my stomach, just like in our cornfields back home.

The judge blew her whistle.

Tam and I flew onto the course. Tam hurtled through the tire jump, bounded up the steep side of the A-frame, skidding down the other side. He sailed over two jumps, one after the other, like he had angel wings; he was always watching me from the corner of his eye.

Some handlers yell at their dogs the whole time they run the course. Others have all these fancy hand signals, even whistles, telling their dogs where to go and what to do. But me and Tam didn't need any of that. We had a special understanding. All I had to do was shift a shoulder or nod my head a certain way and he understood. Tam always understood.

He flew across the catwalk, charged through the tunnel, bursting out the other end with a bark. He slipped in and out of the weave poles easy as water flowing down a stream.

The end of the course was in sight. All we had left was the teeter-totter and two high jumps. I reckon at that point the crowd was standing and cheering us on, but I didn't hear them. All I knew was me and Tam and the sun shining bright.

We ran to the end of the course and crossed the finish line. Tam leaped into my arms, covering my face with kisses. My heart about burst out of my chest as I looked up at the time clock. We had won.

Mama and I were loading our stuff into the truck when Megan Smoot came sidling over. With one of those big ol' fakey smiles, she said, "Congrats on your first-place win, Abby! You and Sam were just super!"

I glanced over at her. The sun glinting off her braces about put my eyes out. "It's *Tam*, not Sam," I snapped. Which Megan knew, seeing as how we had this exact same conversation at each and every competition.

"Oh right," she said. "Well, anyway, there's going to be a pizza party at my house next weekend for everyone in the Junior Handlers Club. Even though you're *still* not a member, we'd love to have you."

I looked away. "Tam and I might be busy that weekend." Doing what, I didn't know. But I'd rather spend a day in the dentist chair than go to her party.

Megan laughed. "No dogs, silly. This is just for us. It'll be fun!"

That sealed the deal. I wasn't going anywhere without Tam.

Megan walked away, swinging her hair this way and that.

"'It'll be *fun*,'" I said in a high, needley voice that to my mind sounded like a bothersome mosquito.

"Well, it might be," Mama said.

I snorted. "I went to her party last year, remember? The last thing I would call it is fun." All the kids in the Junior Handlers Club were from cities and big towns like Asheville, Hendersonville, and Weaverville. They talked to me like I was a stupid little hillbilly kid. Mama didn't understand what that felt like. She'd grown up in a city.

But Tam understood. Tam always understood.

Mama pushed the hair out of her eyes. "Wouldn't hurt for you to make some two-footed friends, you know. Everybody needs friends."

"I got Olivia," I said. "The last time I checked, she had two feet."

Mama smiled. "Olivia's a fine friend too. But it wouldn't hurt for you to broaden your horizons a little. Meet some kids outside Harmony Gap."

I lifted Tam into his crate in the back of the truck. I hated this part, the way he looked at me with those chocolate-brown eyes like I was doing the worst possible thing. But Mama was real particular about her brand-new truck. If it had been Daddy's old van, Tam would sit right up front with us.

I fiddled with the latch on the crate door. It was so old and rusted, it didn't work worth squat.

"Let's get going, Abby. I want to drive a little ways on the Blue Ridge Parkway before we stop for the night. It'd be nice to see some fall colors."

I stretched my fingers through the wire of the crate door. I stroked the white star on the top of his head.

Tam licked my fingertips. "Sorry, boy," I said. "You know how Mama is." I slipped him a piece of cheese and scratched his small, fine head.

"Come on, Abby," Mama called, leaning out the truck window.

"Okay, okay," I said.

I gave Tam one last scratch behind his ear in that special spot he loves. "Don't worry, Tam," I said. "In no time we'll be home and everything will be just fine."

CHAPTER 2

Tam

The dog waited. He watched the girl walk to the side of the truck and open the car door. Surely she would come back, open the crate, and lift him into her arms. Then everything would be as it should be.

The truck door slammed. The engine rumbled to life. Tam whined, pawed at the wire door. Where was the girl, *his* girl, with her smell of grass and soap and sweat and the sound of her heart beating against his ear? Although a mere four feet separated dog and girl, to Tam, it might as well have been four hundred miles.

The crate rocked and jiggled on the flatbed of the truck. Tam sighed and then lay down on the old towel covering the bottom of the crate to sleep.

* * *

Something jolted Tam awake. The truck screamed in alarm. It swerved one way and then the other, throwing dog and crate against the metal sides of the truck. The sick smell of burning rubber filled his nose.

Tam yelped, scrambling to keep his footing. A crash, the sound of tearing, splitting metal, shattering glass. The truck careened through thick green walls of rhododendron and laurel. The sound of the girl's and the woman's cries filled him with fear.

Then the dog's world turned upside down. Trees somersaulted overhead; the ground became the sky. Up and up he sailed and tumbled through the air, down a steep embankment, and away from all he knew.

Silence. Stillness.

Something pulled the dog from the dark place. It was her voice, calling him. She was frightened. He must go to her. Now.

Tam stood. Pain seared through his shoulder, his hip. His feet tangled in the old towel the girl had placed in the crate. His legs would not hold him.

He whined, listened again for her voice. All he heard were small rustlings in the undergrowth, the snap of a twig. The sharp smell of water rose from below.

Tam shivered. The memory of his girl's cries filled him with panic.

Tam barked, clawed at the side of the crate. He pushed his weight against the wire door. Resting precariously on a rock ledge, it tipped forward. Dog and crate slid down the rock face, splashing into the creek below. The current grabbed them and spun them away from the bank.

Icy water rushed into the vents of the crate. Tam hated water. He did not like to swim. He did not like to get his feet wet. Now the water rose up his legs. Horror bit deep into his soul. Tam cowered in one corner of the crate, then clawed at the door again, tearing his nails and pads.

He pushed against the door. Rust and age had kept the latch from sliding into place. It gave way. He plunged into dark, rushing water. Although the water pushed him away, the tags on his collar caught in the wire door, holding him fast.

Tam pulled hard. He worked his head furiously side to side. Water rushed into his mouth and up his nose. Bracing his front paws against the crate, he dipped his head and pulled back, popping free of the collar and the tags that told everyone who he was and that he belonged to her. The current grabbed him, tumbling him down-river, away from the crate and the collar and the memory of the warm, soft bed he shared with his girl.

CHAPTER 3

Abby

I rose up and up from dark, watery sleep, my heart beating a million miles a minute. The light was bright. I tried hard to focus my eyes, to see all the familiar things in my room. My rock and feather collection on top of my bookcase. My story maps pinned to the wall. My old guitar. The trophies and ribbons Tam and I won the last two years. And Tam's warm body pressed next to mine.

Tam! Right there on the edge of my brain . . . I'd had a dream, something bad had happened to him. I couldn't quite grab it and remember, but I had to.

I tried to sit up. "Oh!" I cried.

A warm hand pushed me back. "Lie still, Abby." Mama's voice.

Slowly she came into focus. Her arm was in a bright

blue sling, the other arm bandaged in layers of white gauze. One side of her face was swollen and bruised. The scariest part, though, was the look in her eyes.

"What . . . where am I?" I asked, trying to sit up again.

"You're in the hospital, Abby. We were in a bad accident. Don't you remember?" She smoothed the hair back from my forehead like she'd done a million times before when I'd been sick or sad.

"Daddy's on his way," Mama said. "He should be here anytime." She talked faster and faster. "As soon as the doctors say you can leave, we're going home. And not on the Parkway this time. I knew that was a bad idea. I don't know what I was thinking—"

"Tam!" I said, cutting her off. Panic turned my insides to ice. "Where's Tam?"

She sighed and looked away.

"Mama?"

Her eyes filled with tears. A fist grabbed my heart and squeezed hard. One thing about my mama is that she *never* cries. Not when her favorite llama died this past spring; not when she cut her finger open slicing apples for the pie I wanted; not when Daddy's gone off for weeks and weeks with his band.

She pulled up a chair and sat down. She made little folds over and over in my blanket. "When we swerved off the road and went through the guardrail, Tam's crate was thrown from the back of the truck."

I squeezed my eyes shut. Little flashes were coming back to me: the first-place medal Tam and I won in the agility trial. The winding road high up on the Virginia end of the Blue Ridge Parkway. A sudden flash of brown. The truck going every which way. Then . . . blackness.

Tears trickled down my face. "Is he dead?" I whispered, hardly able to get the words out.

No answer. I opened my eyes. "Mama?"

"I don't know, Abby."

"What do you mean, you don't know?"

Mama looked at me with her gray eyes. The same eyes as mine. "I say I don't know because his crate was thrown from the truck. And he was in it."

"Didn't you look for him?"

She walked to the window. "Abby, we were in a very bad accident. We were both out for I don't know how long. When I came to, there was blood everywhere . . . you weren't responding." She turned her back to me. In a voice I could hardly make out, she said, "I didn't know if . . ."

"But Tam—"

She turned around, cut me off. "My first priority was *you*, Abby. To be honest, I didn't even think about Tam. I had to get help as fast as possible."

"He could still be out there!" I cried. "He could be hurt!"

"I told the police about Tam," Mama said. "They

12

promised to send a couple of officers and Animal Control to look for him."

"And have they looked?" I asked.

Mama grew still. "They haven't found him yet, but they promised they'll keep looking."

I couldn't breathe. Every crack and crevice in my brain worked to put all the pieces together.

Just then, the door swung open. Daddy's wide shoulders filled the doorway, his wild hair flying around him. Worry pulled his eyebrows together when he saw Mama. But when he saw me, his face went white.

In two long strides, he crossed the room and gathered me carefully in his arms. For the first time, I let myself cry. "Oh, Daddy," I sobbed into his shirt. "I've lost Tam."

I grabbed on to my father's hand. "We got to go back up there, Daddy, and look for him. He could be hurt bad."

He looked at Mama, eyebrows raised.

Mama shook her head. "Abby, you not only have a concussion, but your ankle's got a big crack in it. The doctor's not going to release you today."

"I feel fine," I said, pushing the covers off. "Tam's probably right there where we crashed, waiting for us in that crate."

Mama and Daddy exchanged another one of those looks. Daddy said, "Peanut, it's been a whole day since the accident."

13

How could that be? "Then we *have* to get up there. He's looking for me. I can feel it."

"We can't, Abby," Mama said. "The doctor says I have to be in Asheville day after tomorrow to meet with a specialist about my shoulder at the hospital there."

I was trapped, but I had to get to Tam!

Mama turned to Daddy. "Could you drive up there, Ian, and take a look around? I can give you directions."

"No," I said. "I have to go too." I swung my legs over the edge of the bed. The pain about made me throw up.

Mama clamped her good hand on my shoulder. Hard. Her face was gray. "Be still, Abby. First things first. Let's talk to the doctor and see when he thinks you can be released. As soon as he says you can go, we'll head back up to the Parkway and look for Tam."

"But—" I started to protest.

Daddy placed a finger on my lips. "Hush now, honey. Who knows? Maybe someone's found him already. He has ID tags on his collar."

"And he's microchipped," my mother added.

"Besides, he was in the crate," Daddy said. "He's not going anywhere soon."

They both smiled, but their eyes said they didn't really believe what they were saying.

14

CHAPTER 4

Tam

Sunlight burned off the mist hovering over the creek. By the time it reached the bed Tam had made under a fallen birch, the forest had been awake for a long time. Squirrels and chipmunks busily gathered acorns to store against the winter months ahead. Red foxes lined their burrows with leaves, and geese passed overhead, pointing the way south. Life in the Appalachian Mountains in late October was a race against time.

Tam knew nothing of the ice and snow just weeks away. As he tried to rise from the damp earth, all he knew was how much his bruised, cold body hurt and how hungry he was.

With a groan, Tam limped down to the creek and

drank, careful not to get his feet wet. He lifted his head, nose reading the damp air crisscrossed with scents. Any other time, Tam would have followed his nose through the streams of scent, like a fish hooked on a line.

But Tam was hurt. And a hurt dog knows only one thing to do: be still.

Tam took one last drink, then limped back to his shelter. He lowered himself to the ground with a whimper. He didn't stir when a large gray squirrel ran back and forth across the fallen tree. He slept as two white-tailed deer slipped down to drink from the creek. And as the moon rose over the ridge and a great horned owl hunted the far meadow, Tam dreamed of hot gravy and chunks of beef set before him next to the woodstove in his home with his girl.

CHAPTER 5

Abby

Daddy sucked in his breath. "Good Lord." He stared at the crumpled guardrail and the skid marks of our tires.

"Tam," I said. "Remember?"

"Right," Daddy said.

It had been a whole day before the doctor let me out of that putrid hospital. Time to find Tam was a-wasting.

Daddy and Mama got out of the van. I opened the back door and tried to maneuver the crutches in front of me. Mama hurried over. "No, Abby, you stay here. The road's too narrow. Daddy and I will call him."

"But he needs to hear *my* voice," I said. "If he's scared or hurt, he might not answer you."

With a sigh, Mama helped me stand and brace myself against the car. Filling my lungs with hope, I cried out as loud as I could, "Tam! Come here, Tam!" We listened for any sound—a bark, a jingle of tags. Nothing. I called again. And again and again and again. Until my voice was broken.

Daddy studied the place where the truck had plowed through the trees and bushes. Shattered limbs and glass marked the path. "Seems like the crate would have been thrown down this way," he said. "I'll take a look."

"The crate should be easy to spot," Mama said.

Daddy disappeared through the trees. I held my breath so I could hear him call, *I found him! He's okay!*

My all-time record for holding my breath was one minute and forty-three seconds. I broke that record and then some that day. But all I heard was wind and birds and Mama tapping her finger on the door of the van.

She reached out and pushed my hand away from my mouth. "Stop chewing your hair, Abby."

I dropped the wet end of my braid. "It's been hours, Mama. What's taking him so long?"

Mama looked at her watch. "It's only been fifteen minutes. I imagine he'll be back any second."

Daddy scrambled over the guardrail. His face was flushed and sad. He shook his head.

"No sign of him, peanut."

"Not even his crate?" Mama asked.

Daddy wiped his hands on his jeans. "Trouble is, the embankment goes right to the edge of a little cliff. Then it drops straight down to the creek. There's not a shore or anything. Just rocks and a lot of water."

A huge lump lodged in my throat. I blinked back tears.

"Daddy, there must be a place farther along the creek to get down to the shore," I said.

"I was thinking the same thing," he said.

We drove a ways up the road. Daddy climbed the guardrail and went off into the woods while I called Tam. Nothing.

Then we drove down the road and did the same thing. I called, waited, and listened. The sun topped the trees. After a time, the sun stood straight over us. Maybe it was a good sign Daddy was gone so long. Mama lay down in the backseat. She didn't look so good. I stayed beside the van, watching the spot where Daddy would surely appear— with Tam.

But he didn't. He walked out of the woods alone. "I'm sorry, honey," he said.

"But Tam has to be *somewhere*," I said.

Mama sat up. "Okay then, let's head up to the Visitor Center and talk to the rangers."

I knew she was right, but I didn't want to leave. Surely Tam would come back here, if he could.

Putting his arm around my shoulders, Daddy said, "Come on, peanut. Let's go."

I jerked away from Daddy's arm and pushed off on my crutches. I got to going pretty fast, once I got the rhythm down.

"Abigail Andrea Whistler, you stop right now!" Mama called.

"I've got to find him, Mama," I called back over my shoulder. "I just know he's—"

The tip of my left crutch missed the edge of the road. I pitched head over heels into the gravel. Daddy was pulling me into his big arms before I had time to blink.

Mama brushed the rocks and dirt from my face. She grabbed the end of one of my braids and gave it a shake. "Honestly, Abby. When God handed out stubborn genes, you got the mother lode."

Daddy lifted me into his arms. "Come on, Abby honey. Tam's not here."

CHAPTER 6

Tam

Tam lapped water from the creek, eyes closed. His shoulder and hip still ached. His stomach grumbled. He had not eaten since the morning of the accident.

Then he heard it. So faint at first, even Tam, with his keen hearing, wasn't sure it was real. He threw his ears forward, water dripping from his muzzle.

Silence.

Just as he lowered his head, he heard it, stronger this time. Every muscle in his body tensed. Fainter than any human ear could possibly hear, Tam heard her voice. "Tam! Tam!"

Tam barked once, twice, then listened again. Her call came from the north. He fixed on the direction, barked again, and picked his way along the creek bank. He did not know that between him and the girl lay miles of rhododendron and mountain laurel so thick a person couldn't push through it. He could not know that it would take hours to work his way back upstream.

All he knew was she was calling. For all the years he could remember, this voice was his world, his compass. And when the person he loves most in the world calls, a dog can do nothing but go.

CHAPTER 7

Abby

"I heard about your accident," the ranger at the Humpback Rocks Visitor Center said after Mama explained who we were. "We get deer-related accidents up here all the time. You'd think they'd learn."

I wasn't sure if he was talking about the deer or the drivers.

I cleared my throat. "My dog was in a crate in the back of the truck. When we hit the guardrail, he was thrown out."

"We just drove back to the spot where they went off the road," Daddy said. "I looked all around. We even drove a half mile back up the road and went down to the creek there, and the other way too. I didn't see any sign of him or the crate."

The ranger sighed. "Folks lose dogs up here a lot."

I thrust the flyers with Tam's photo at the man. "This is Tam. He's not just any dog. He's a champion." *And my best friend*.

The ranger studied the picture and smiled. "A little Lassie."

"You're familiar with Shetland sheepdogs?" Mama asked.

"My wife grew up with them. She loves these little dogs. We'd have one if our son wasn't so allergic."

Daddy placed the rest of the flyers on the desk. "Any chance you could post these around for us?"

"We're offering a reward," I said.

The ranger ran his finger along the edge of the picture. "Agility champion, huh? I seen that on TV once. My wife watches Animal Planet all the time. Generally speaking, we don't post private notices, though."

Mama said, "He's *very*, *very* important to my daughter, sir. And to us."

He looked me over with my crutches and Mama with her bandaged arm and complicated sling. "There's some bathrooms and picnic areas fairly close. I reckon I can post a few of these around."

Daddy's face broke open with relief. "We'd really appreciate it. We're heading home, but if anyone finds him or knows anything about him, they can call us collect. The phone number is right on the flyer."

The ranger glanced down at our number below Tam's picture. "That a North Carolina number?"

Daddy nodded. "About forty-five miles south of Asheville in a little place called Harmony Gap. We live just outside of there in Wild Cat Cove."

The ranger whistled. "The other end of the Blue Ridge Parkway. That's a heck of a ways from up here in Virginia."

"If somebody finds him, we'll come get him right away," I said. It couldn't be that far.

The ranger sighed and gathered up the flyers. "Let's hope someone does and soon, honey. Winter's not far off up here. Once it sets in, most of the Parkway closes down. Nobody will be back up until spring."

My heart dropped down to my sneakers.

After Daddy settled my leg on pillows in the backseat of the van, I said, "Can we go back and look one more time?"

"No, Abby," Mama said.

"But he might be there."

"It's almost ten miles back. Besides, it'll be dark soon."

"So?" I said, not caring how much Mama hates it when I say this. "We could spend the night in Waynesboro again, come back up tomorrow and look some more."

This time Daddy turned around. "Abby, we need to get both of you *home*. Your mama has to see that doctor in Asheville tomorrow, and your grandmother's worried sick.

"Besides," he said, rubbing the back of his neck, "we just don't have the money to be spending on all these nights in motels."

"But Daddy, we can't just leave without Tam. He's—"

His blue eyes, the eyes that always laughed, turned hard. "A dog, Abby. He's a dog. I know how much he means to you, but you and your mother are more important to me right now."

Daddy turned around, steered the van onto the road.

I was so shocked by my daddy's hard heart, I felt like I'd been slapped full in the face.

"I bet by the time we get home, someone will have called," Mama said. Touching Daddy's shoulder, she added, "And I'm thinking we'll try and get back up here in the next weekend or two."

"But Mama, if he's trapped in that crate, he'll starve or thirst to death."

Daddy glanced at me in the rearview mirror. "It's the best we can do right now, sugar. Besides, Tam's a tough little dog."

Every foot, every bit of mile we went down that road tore at my soul. "Promise?" I asked. "Promise we'll come back?"

Mama reached back and squeezed my hand. "We'll try."

We took the turnoff for Roanoke. The forest and trees closed behind us like a green, secret wall.

CHAPTER 8

Tam

Tam sniffed the spot where Abby had stood just hours before. He smelled the woman and the big man too, but he drank in the scent of his girl. It was not quite her usual smell of grass and apples and her body's own unique mixture, though. There was a smell of pain and fear he did not understand.

What Tam did understand was she had been there, so he must wait. Often he had waited, long spaces of time, when she left just as the sun topped the ridge and did not return until the sun's shadows grew long. But she always came back. The big bus would rattle up to the mailbox at the bottom of the hill. His girl would run down the bus steps calling, "Tam! Come on, Tam!"—the sweetest sound the sheltie had heard all day. He would launch himself off the porch, as if he had wings, and race down the hill. When he and his girl were together, everything was as it should be.

Tam sighed, lay down next to the spot beside the road that held the strongest scent of her, and closed his eyes. The scent of girl and grass and water carried him home.

For two days, Tam stayed close to the spot with her scent. The occasional car passed by, and always Tam watched from beneath the undergrowth. But the cars never stopped.

On the third day, rain pushed Tam away from the roadside and into the deep forest. Even under the thick canopy of mountain laurel and impenetrable mesh of honeysuckle vine, the rain found him, soaking his dense coat.

Tam groaned and curled tighter into himself. He shivered as the rain and wind howled overhead. His stomach growled. Another day passed without food.

The rain finally stopped. Tam climbed back up the bank to the road. He sniffed the spot where he had smelled the girl. The smell of her and the woman and the big man were gone. As hard as his nose worked the ground, he could not find the scent of her. All he smelled were rotting leaves and the acrid scent of wet asphalt. He stood by the side of the road, bewildered and heartsick. Without the scent of her to guide him, what was he to do? He trembled with utter aloneness.

The shadows of the late afternoon grew long. Something deep within him stirred.

Geese know without being told when it is time to head south for the winter. Foxes know when it is time to dig dens for the babies to come. And Tam knew it was time. Time to find his girl.

Tam scented the air, searching. He trotted north up the road. He stopped, then walked a little farther. He paused and sniffed. The north held nothing for him. He turned and trotted south. The farther he went, the stronger that direction pulled him, true as the needle on a compass. South was the way he must go. Soon, he would see his beloved girl, and everything would be as it should be.

He could not know the many miles and vast wilderness that lay between him and his home with the girl. A dog does not measure distance in miles or even days. A dog only knows that every footfall, every heartbeat, brings him closer to his heart's desire. Anyone seeing Tam trotting with his easy gait along the side of the road would see a dog going home.

CHAPTER 9

Abby

I sat on the window seat in my room, listening to the quiet. No jingling of tags on Tam's collar, no click of his toenails on the pinewood floors. Nothing but putrid silence. I felt sick all the way through. The past two days we'd been home felt like twenty.

My eyes settled on my old guitar sitting in the corner. I'd hardly touched it in the three years since I'd had Tam, I'd been so busy with him.

Now that my arms and my heart were empty without Tam, I wanted to hold that guitar to me more than anything. I wanted to feel the comfort of its weight and the hum of the strings.

I'd just started to get up when I heard a peck on my

door, and Meemaw opened it. She stood tall and straight as a Carolina pine, her long braid wrapped like a fiery crown on top of her head.

"Abby honey, you got a visitor," she said.

I plopped back down and in stepped my friend Olivia McButtars, the littlest, shyest, smartest girl in the whole sixth grade. Maybe even the world.

Olivia peered at me from behind her big glasses. Most of the kids at school said her pale green eyes were creepy. They do seem to look right into a person's soul. But to my way of thinking, that wasn't a bad thing.

Olivia crossed the room and sat beside me. She sighed. "I'm sorry about Tam." No small talk for Olivia. She cut right to the chase.

"I just don't know what to do or what to think," I said around a big knot of tears in my throat. "And that makes me so mad, I could spit."

Olivia touched the back of my hand light as a butter-fly. "I know exactly what you mean."

And she wasn't just saying that to be nice, neither. She really did know.

Right after Christmastime last year, Olivia moved to Harmony Gap from way up in Baltimore, Maryland. She moved here to live with her granddaddy, Mr. Alphus Singer, after her mama and daddy disappeared out over the Pacific Ocean in one of those little-bitty airplanes. Olivia told me once she reckoned her mama was now a mermaid, something her mother always wanted to be. And that gave Olivia a measure of comfort.

We sat there on the window seat for a long time, not saying a word, just listening to the wind in the trees, thunder rolling around in the far mountains.

Finally I asked, "Olivia, do you think there's any chance Tam's still alive?" Olivia would be honest with me, I knew.

She didn't say anything for a long moment. Her eyes drifted around my room, taking in the photographs and drawings of Tam, all my special, handmade story maps of the things me and Tam had done and the adventures I had planned for us.

Then she turned and looked directly into my eyes. "My mom often said love creates miracles."

And that was all Olivia had to say about that. And it was all I needed to hear.

After she left, I hobbled across the room and picked up my old guitar. It'd been my grandpa Bill's pride and joy. I don't remember Grandpa Bill all that well. We moved in here with Meemaw after he was killed in the sawmill accident. But all my memories of him are wrapped around him and this guitar.

I carried it back over to my bed, ran my hand across the strings. I hugged the guitar against my stomach and felt the chords thrum against my heart. I closed my eyes, dug way back in my memory, and sang the first song I came across:

> *This little light of mine, I'm gonna let it shine.*
> *This little light of mine, I'm gonna let it shine.*

The next day, me and Daddy bumped along the red clay road that took us to Harmony Gap. Daddy hummed under his breath.

"Daddy," I said, "we've been home for days now. When're we going back up to Virginia to look for Tam?"

Daddy stopped humming and rubbed the back of his neck like he always does when he doesn't know the answer to something. "I'm not exactly sure, peanut. Soon."

"Mama promised," I reminded him.

"I know she did," Daddy said with a frown. "But you've both had doctor appointments and whatnot. Plus she's had to go back to work, you know. She can't just take off work whenever she feels like it."

I thought my head would explode like a volcano. "She promised!"

Daddy shot me a look. "I know what was said, Abby. I was there too, remember? And what she said was we'd *try* our best to get back up there."

"Doesn't seem to me like there's a whole heck of a lot of trying going on," I muttered.

"Besides," Daddy said, ignoring me, "you've been calling that ranger station every day at least once. They know to watch out for him."

Daddy swung the truck into the parking space in front of the post office. "Let's get these packages of yarn mailed off to your mama's customers." He scooped up a big stack of boxes labeled *Whistler Farm Specialty Fibers*.

Old Mr. McGruber was the only one behind the high wooden desk, which accounted for the line of people waiting to do their business. Mr. McGruber saw it as his God-given duty to ask after every customer's health and their family's health and all their animals' health. And then he told them about his.

I sighed and shifted my weight on those crutches. Daddy smiled down at me and winked.

"Hey there, Abby." A hand touched my shoulder.

Mr. Morgan's kind eyes took in my banged-up head, crutches, and cast.

"Hey, Mr. Morgan," I said. Me and Tam took our first agility class from him.

"I sure was sorry to hear about your accident," he said, shaking his head. "And about Tam. He was a real special little dog."

I stood up as straight as I could and looked him directly in the eye. "We're heading back up there in the next day or two to get him."

Mr. Morgan's bushy black eyebrows pulled together. "Someone found him?"

Daddy shook his head.

"Not exactly yet," I said. "But he's up there waiting for me. I can feel it."

Mr. Morgan and Daddy passed one of those looks between them.

"Well, I hope that's true, Abby honey," Mr. Morgan said, patting my shoulder.

At supper that night, I said, "Mama, are we going back up to Virginia this weekend to find Tam?"

Everyone stopped chewing. Daddy and Meemaw looked at Mama.

Mama set down her fork and ran her napkin across her lips. "Well, I hadn't had time to think about it."

"You promised, remember?" I said, not looking at Daddy.

Mama nodded. "Yes, I said we'd do our best to get back up there." She looked at Daddy. "What do you think, Ian?"

Daddy frowned. "It's a long ways back up to Virginia. Even if we made a three-day weekend of it, it'd mostly be driving."

"It's not that far," I said. "We could be back up there in no time."

Mama and Daddy looked at me like I'd grown two

heads. "Abby honey, it's well over four hundred miles from here to where y'all crashed on the Parkway," Daddy said.

I about spit my peas across the table. "Four hundred miles? That can't be right! We made it home in no time, and . . ."

"You slept most of the way back," Mama pointed out.

I looked at Meemaw. She nodded.

"We've been calling the ranger station every day, though," Mama said.

"It's not the same," I snapped.

"Abby," Daddy warned.

"No, Abby's right. It's not the same," Mama said.

I about fell out of my chair in pure astonishment.

"I did say we'd try our best to get back up there. I always keep my word."

Daddy sighed. "All right. I reckon it won't hurt to take a quick trip back up there. We'll leave Friday and come back Sunday."

"Can't we come back Monday?" I asked.

"No, Abby. We've let you stay out of school this week, but you can't afford to miss any more."

I was sorely tempted to point out that until just a couple years ago, they homeschooled me. But Meemaw is forever reminding me you catch more flies with honey than with vinegar. So instead I smiled sweet as coconut-cream pie and said, "Thank you, Mama. I just know we'll find him this time."

That was on Wednesday.

On Thursday Daddy's van broke down in Asheville.

"I'm sorry, peanut," Daddy said when he finally got a ride home that night. "I know you had your heart set on leaving tomorrow for Virginia, but we don't have a way to get up there."

"We have to, Daddy! Can't we borrow a car or something?"

Daddy rubbed a greasy hand across his tired face. "I got to get our van fixed. Until your mama gets her new truck, we're stuck."

"But Daddy—"

"Enough buts," he said. "I'm just as frustrated as you are. The band is scheduled to head out for a bunch of gigs next week. I need that van working." He sighed a long, deep-down sigh. "Lord knows where the money's going to come from to fix it."

He pulled back the covers and patted the bed. "Maybe once your mama gets her new truck, y'all can make a trip back up. Until then, we'll keep calling and praying."

I burrowed down into the warm smell of Tam in my blankets. Ginseng the cat purred on the pillow next to me.

Fighting back an ocean of tears, I said, "I'll never give up on finding Tam, Daddy. Never."

CHAPTER 10

Tam

As the days passed, hunger as strong as his need for the girl drove Tam. The light step that had carried him for days and miles grew heavier. Still, at precisely three thirty every afternoon, the hunger to see his girl propelled him south along the Parkway.

Tam nosed a paper bag blown to the side of the road. All he found were two dried-up french fries and a shriveled piece of lettuce. He licked a smear of ketchup from the inside of the bag and moved on.

He watched squirrels and chipmunks stuff acorns and berries in their bulging cheeks. But the acorns were bitter, the berries tough and sour. He picked at whatever green grass he could find, but it wasn't enough. Tam was starving.

* * *

On a cloudy late afternoon, a scent pulled Tam to a place where people had been. He nosed around the picnic tables dotting the meadow. He found a few crusts of bread and some potato chips, but as hard as he searched, he found nothing else. As dusk descended on the mountain, Tam scratched out a bed beneath a picnic table. Misery filled his stomach. A small brick bathroom squatted to the side of the parking lot. A flyer with Tam's face flapped in the evening breeze.

A crash woke him. Peering through the light rain, Tam saw the black mask of a raccoon as he crawled across an overturned garbage can. The raccoon pried and pulled at the metal top with his humanlike hands, methodically working the edges of the lid. Then, bracing his powerful back legs against the bottom of the trash can, he tugged at the top edge until the top popped off.

Tam's nose filled with the scent of food.

The raccoon dug through the garbage. He pulled out half-eaten sandwiches, apple cores, hot dog buns, fried chicken remains, and a carton of old potato salad. An empty soda can rolled down the parking lot.

Tam crept from under the picnic table and moved toward the garbage can and the wonderful smell of food. He knew about garbage. He had gotten in trouble more than once for tipping over the tall can in the kitchen. The old woman had scolded him and shut him outside. After the girl had called him "bad dog" in her angry voice, he'd never gotten into the garbage again.

But now Tam was starving. And as much as the memory of displeasing his girl held him back, the hunger clawing at his stomach pushed him forward.

The raccoon sorted busily through the trash. He didn't hear Tam until he barked a friendly *woof.* Tam wagged his tail hopefully. He'd never met a raccoon before, but this one reminded him of the cats at home.

The raccoon hunched over his prize, growling and hissing. Sometimes the cats hissed too, but it was just part of the game they played. Tam wagged his tail again, took one step forward. The raccoon bristled. He pulled his lips back, flashing sharp, white teeth.

The sheltie barked, thrusting his head forward.

Quick as a flash, the raccoon raked his claws across Tam's face, barely missing his eye. Tam smelled blood. This had never happened with the cats.

Tam retreated to his shelter under the picnic table, his sorrowful eyes abrim with misery.

After a time, the creature waddled off. Tam watched the garbage. Once he was certain the raccoon was not coming back, he returned to the can. All that remained were a few chicken bones, a watermelon rind, and half a hot dog bun. The memory of his girl's voice saying "Bad dog, Tam!" faded with every bite he took.

It rained hard for two days. Autumnal winds stripped the last of the bright yellow leaves from the trees.

Tam pushed farther into the corner of the brick bathroom, watching wind blow sheets of rain past the doorway. What little garbage there had been in the cans, Tam had eaten. He licked a cut on his pad, then sighed. He slept as the day slipped from gray to black.

Headlights swung into the parking lot, settling just above Tam. Laughter and the slam of a car door startled him from sleep. Music throbbed from the car.

Tam sat up, nose sorting through the scents of rain, wet earth, sweet smoke, and people. Unsteady footsteps stumbled toward Tam. He whined uncertainly. Something about the car, the laughter, and the human coming toward him didn't smell right. Still, people meant food. His instinct told him to run and hide before anyone saw him; his stomach told him to stay.

Too late, Tam decided to honor his instinct to run.

Just as he started to scoot around the doorway, long legs and big feet blocked his way. He scrambled to the corner.

"Holy crap!" a voice cried. "It's a fox in here!" Legs and feet stumbled backward, tripped over a tree root, body

41

sprawling. Hoots of laughter from the car, angry voice from the human on the wet ground.

Tam crouched, muscles tensed. Just as he was about to shoot through the doorway, a bottle exploded above his head. Foul-smelling liquid and glass rained down upon him.

The human pulled himself up off the ground. "Git, you no-good vermin!"

Tam cowered, looking frantically for a way out.

The man moved toward him, smelling of anger. For the first time in Tam's life, he bared his teeth and growled at a human.

The man stopped just short of the doorway. Tam growled louder, warning him away.

"Why, you no-good chicken killer," the human growled back. He grabbed a rock and hurled it at the dog. The stone ricocheted like gunshot off the brick wall. Tam yelped in alarm.

The man turned his back to Tam and called through the rain, "Hey, Beattie, you got your shotgun? I got me a fox cornered over here I need to take care of."

When the human looked back, the bathroom was empty.

CHAPTER 11

Abby

As soon as school let out Monday afternoon, I went to the front office.

The secretary, Miss Peasly, sorted papers behind the counter. I cleared my throat.

Miss Peasly looked up and smiled. "Well, hi there, Abby. Did you have a good day at school?"

"Yes, ma'am." The first lie.

"That's nice, honey," she said, picking up her papers.

I shifted my weight on my crutches. "Um . . ."

She looked up at me again. "Is there something you need, Abby?"

"Yes, ma'am," I said. "I need a ride to the bus station."

She took her glasses off and let them hang from strings

against her big bosom. "Why in the world would you need a ride to the bus station?" she asked.

I swallowed. "I . . . I have a relative coming in on the bus this afternoon. From Virginia. I have to meet him there." The second lie.

She puckered up her lips. "Why don't your mama or daddy pick him up?"

My hands started to sweat, and my stomach itched. This lying was hard. "My mama's going to meet us both there and carry us on back to the house. I'm—I'm just going to surprise her. I mean him."

Miss Peasly studied me for a minute too long. I about melted in a puddle of relief when she said, "I guess I can do that. I have to go right by there on my way home." She put the papers away in the file cabinet. "Give me just a minute and I'll run you over there."

I crutched over to the bench where kids usually sat when they were waiting to see the principal. Bad kids. I felt like a bad kid too, telling all those lies to a nice person like Miss Peasly.

I pulled the bus schedule I'd printed out on the school library printer from my backpack. I had to catch the three forty-five bus to Asheville if I had any hope of getting the bus up to Waynesboro, Virginia, tonight.

I glanced at the big clock on the wall. Right about now, the bus to my house would be pulling out of the school yard. I wished Miss Peasly would hurry up.

"Let's go, sugar," Miss Peasly said, swinging a big plastic purse over her shoulder.

I'm here to tell you, Miss Peasly is the slowest driver on God's green earth. She drove with one arm hanging out the car window, waving to anybody and everybody, like we had all the time in the world. Which I surely did not.

"When do you get that cast off?" she asked me.

"Couple weeks," I said. At which point, I would be back from Virginia with Tam.

"You settling into school okay this year? I know it's been a hard adjustment after being homeschooled and all."

I just shrugged. Then, remembering my manners, I said, "Yes, ma'am."

She smiled over at me. "It must have been exciting traveling with your daddy's band, the Clear Creek Boys."

I'd never really thought about it being exciting or not. It was all I'd known since I was first born, traveling all over the place in our old camper van surrounded by music.

When I didn't answer, she said, "I know your grandmamma was thankful when y'all moved in after your granddaddy died so unexpectedly. That place of hers way up in Wild Cat Cove is too isolated for a woman alone."

Finally, the Greyhound bus station came into view.

Before she came to a full stop, I unbuckled my seat belt. "I surely do appreciate the ride," I said. I swung open the car door, scooted my crutches out in front of me, and put on my pack.

I slammed the car door shut. Miss Peasly stretched across the car seat and looked at me like she was trying to think of what else to say. She opened that puckery mouth of hers. "Abby, are you sure—"

I waved. "Thanks again," I called as I crutched as fast as I could into the bus station.

The bus station was practically empty. An old man in overalls slept sitting up on the bench by the Coke machine; a woman fussed with her cranky baby.

I marched as best I could up to the ticket window. An old man looked up from a paperback book.

"Can I help you?" he asked.

In my oldest voice, I said, "I'd like to purchase a ticket to Asheville, North Carolina." I said it just like I bought bus tickets all the time.

He pushed his glasses up on his nose and leaned forward to get a better look at me. "You would, would you?"

I tried my best to look taller with those stupid crutches. "Yes, sir, I would. I got to go up and see my grandmamma. She's sick." This time, the lie slid off my tongue easy as hot butter.

He leaned out a little farther and looked around the room. "Anyone traveling with you, young lady?"

"No, sir," I said. Which wasn't exactly a lie. "But my

46

granddaddy'll meet my bus in Asheville."

The clock in his office ticked. We looked at each other. Finally he sighed and said, "That'll be forty dollars and sixty cents. Next bus is in fifteen minutes."

I counted out some of the money I'd saved from our win at the agility competition. I surely hoped the rest would buy my bus ticket to Virginia.

After I got my ticket, I bought a Coke from the machine. Mama never let me have Cokes. She said they eat the enamel off your teeth. I figured she'd never know. Besides, I needed lots of brainpower to figure out just what I was going to do once I got to Virginia.

I sat on a bench away from the fussy baby and the snoring man. Fifteen minutes. I'd just make it out of town before Meemaw realized I wasn't coming home.

I took a swallow of Coke. It burned my throat. Maybe Mama was right.

I set the Coke on the floor and unzipped my pack. Instead of all my schoolbooks, notebooks, and stuff, I had: a clean shirt, a clean pair of underwear, a whistle, a picture of Tam, my lucky baseball cap that said *Shelties Rule!*, the lunch Mama packed that I never ate, my old beat-up copy of *The Secret Garden*, which I must've read a million times, and my map-drawing sketch pad.

I glanced at the clock. Just two more minutes. Two more minutes and I'd be on my way to find Tam. I wasn't exactly sure how it was all going to work when I got to Virginia, but I figured it would come to me.

I propped my sketch pad on my knees and studied the map I'd been working on since the accident. I'd drawn in the mountains, and the song Mama and I had been singing, and the winding, winding road, the long shadows of the late afternoon sun, and the deer they said had likely darted in front of the truck. It made me sick to think about it, but I had to draw in Tam and the screeching tires, the smell of burning rubber, shattering glass, how the trees must've somersaulted as he and the crate were thrown from the truck. My heart beat in my throat. Sweat popped out on my arms.

"Abby."

I looked up. My heart froze.

Mama.

I was in for it now. I braced myself for the kind of tongue-lashing only Mama could give.

Instead, she sat down next to me and took my hand. After a long moment she said, "A relative from Virginia, huh?"

I looked away. I guess I wasn't such a good liar.

I thought Mama was going to tell me how sinful it was to lie, how thoughtless I was being.

Instead, she stretched her legs out in front and leaned her head back against the tiled wall.

The silence stretched out between us, taut as a fiddle string.

Then the bus pulled into the front of the station. Above the windshield was the word ASHEVILLE in big letters.

I started to slip my hand out of Mama's. She gripped it tight. "No, Abby," she said.

I watched the people get off the bus. "But Mama, I have a ticket." Mama purely hates wasting money.

She shook her head. "I can't let you go."

My heart pounded as the bus driver helped the woman with the baby onto the bus. The old man gathered up his plastic bags full of who-knows-what and shuffled to the waiting bus.

Mama gripped my hand so hard it hurt.

"Mama, *please*," I said. A tear slipped down my cheek and over my lip. "I got to find him."

Mama wiped the tear away with her thumb. "I understand, Abby. Really I do. But no."

The bus driver mounted the steps and climbed into the driver's seat. Those doors would close any second.

I jerked my hand away and lurched to my feet. I didn't even bother grabbing my pack.

I crutched as fast as I could across the room.

"Abby, stop!" Mama's voice rang out.

I hesitated for a sixteenth of a second, then pushed through the door.

"Wait!" I cried.

The driver revved the engine of the bus. His hand clutched the handle to close the door. He looked from me to Mama.

"Drive on," Mama's voice said behind me. "She's not going."

The door folded shut.

I watched with pure frustration as that bus, the bus that would help me get to Virginia, pulled away. If it weren't for those stupid crutches and the stupider cast, I could have run that bus down.

Mama touched my shoulder. "Time to go home, Abby."

I whirled away from Mama's touch like it was fire.

"Stop it!" I said. "Stop telling me what to do!"

Mama jerked back like I'd slapped her.

"It's all your fault," I said. "If you'd let Tam ride up front with us in your putrid, putrid truck, I'd never have lost Tam! But no, *all* you cared about was how nice your brand-new truck was."

Mama held out a hand like she was trying to ward off a mad dog. "Now, Abby . . ."

A dam burst inside me. "And then you promised we'd go back and look for him, but we haven't, so I have to go myself because none of *you care*!"

Mama folded her arms over her chest. "I do care, Abby. I loved Tam. But I love you more. I have to do what's best for you. Someday you'll understand."

"No I *won't*," I spat. "I won't *ever* understand. All I understand is Tam is out there somewhere, waiting for me. And *you don't care*!"

I stood there trembling like a leaf in the fall wind. I'd never ever talked to an adult like that, much less Mama. She'd probably make me go live in the barn with her precious llamas, or maybe she'd make me walk all the way home. I didn't care. Everything I said was true.

Mama opened her mouth, then closed it. She slumped like somebody had let all the air out of her.

She wiped at the corner of one eye and sniffed. She slung my pack on her good shoulder. "Come on, honey. Let's go home."

I'd gone straight to my room after me and Mama got back from the bus station and didn't come out. My stomach grumbled and growled from missing supper, but I didn't care. Tam was probably starving too.

I got out the map I'd planned to work on during the bus ride to Virginia, when there came a tap on my door.

I gripped my colored pencil tighter. "Go away," I said.

The door swung open anyway. Meemaw stood tall and straight as a pine in the doorway. "I brought you a little bite to eat," she said.

I turned back to my map. "I ain't hungry," I said. Meemaw didn't care how I talked.

She shut the door behind her. "I made you a grilled cheese, all mashed down and gooey the way you like."

My stomach knotted up. I sure did love Meemaw's grilled cheese sandwiches. But still. "No, thank you," I said.

She set the tray with the sandwich and glass of milk on my bed. She picked up the brush off my dresser and came up behind me.

Meemaw worked my braids loose. "Starving yourself won't bring Tam back, Abby."

I closed my eyes against the tears and didn't say anything. That lump in my throat was so big, I couldn't get anything out even if I'd wanted to.

Running the brush from the top of my head and all down my back she said, "You about broke your mama's heart trying to run off like that, honey."

The long strokes of the brush worked out the tangles in my hair and my throat, but I still didn't say anything.

"Your mama's got enough on her mind with your daddy leaving and the money it took to fix that van."

"I don't see why Daddy has to leave again. I thought he'd given up playing music on the road," I said.

Meemaw stopped brushing. "Your daddy's not a stay-by-the-hearth kind of dog. Never has been."

"But Mama says she's just as happy to not be traveling all the time," I pointed out.

Meemaw resumed her brushing. "Yes, she was weary of

life on the road. And it's not a fit life for a child." Meemaw hummed under her breath. "Do you miss the traveling life, Abby?" she asked.

I looked out onto the moonlit fields and dark, dark mountains all around us. I knew every square inch of those eighty acres as well as I knew the color of my eyes and hair and every single freckle. I knew just how the trees whispered to me and Tam on a summer evening, and the best places along Clear Creek to look for salamanders. And that there was no better place to watch for deer than the pond down below the apple orchard.

"No, ma'am," I said. "I'm just as happy we moved in with you. I never want to leave Wild Cat Cove and Harmony Gap."

"That sure is a big ol' yellow moon," Meemaw said in a dreamy kind of voice. "Your grandpa Bill called it a Carolina Moon."

I looked up at Meemaw's face, all faraway-looking like it gets when she talks about my grandpa. I touched her arm to bring her back. "Meemaw, you reckon Tam is looking at this same moon somewhere?"

Meemaw smiled a sad kind of smile. "He just might be, honey. He might be."

CHAPTER 12

Tam

Tam lay in the full sun in a small meadow. The grass was brown now, but at least it was dry. Days of rain and wind had stripped the last of the leaves from the trees. The only color in the forests was the last of the red sumac. Although the nights were cold, Indian summer had found the high country.

Several days had passed since Tam's encounter with the humans at the rest stop. The angry voices, the exploding noises had burned deep into his memory. Humans were to be avoided.

The pinched flanks of the sheltie rose and fell as he slept. His ribs showed through his dirty, matted coat. It had been weeks since the accident, since he had become lost to everything he knew; weeks since he'd had his bowl set down before him by the stove and slept in the warmth of his girl's side.

A raven circled low over the sleeping dog and landed on the branch of a sassafras tree. He cocked his head to one side, then the other, watching the dog in the sun. Curiosity got the best of the raven. He flew down to the grass and hopped to the head of the dog. Tam's nose twitched, ears flicked forward, but his eyes did not open. The raven, always the prankster, snatched a lock of Tam's hair from the tip of his ear.

Tam jerked awake and leaped to his feet. He lunged at the raven, but the bird was too quick. He flew back to the tree and cawed teasingly. Tam danced on his back legs, barking furiously at the raven. The bird plucked twigs and dead, mitten-shaped leaves from the sassafras tree, pelting the dog below.

Tam shook himself and lay back down. He had every intention of ignoring the bird.

The raven would have none of it. He pushed off the limb and soared over the sheltie, snatching at the top of Tam's head with his claws. In the blink of an eye, Tam was on his feet, racing across the meadow after the bird, barking. The raven cawed and taunted him.

The chase was on. Tam leaped over logs, wove through the underbrush, raced across a fallen tree bridging the stream. For the first time in weeks, he forgot the hunger, the fear, the loneliness, and the burning drive to go south. He was doing what he did best, what he'd trained every day to do: cover the obstacle course as quickly as possible.

But this time, as Tam sailed over the last jump and tore around the corner of a blueberry patch, the girl was not there calling his name, arms open. Instead, he ran right into the huge, stinking hulk of a black bear browsing lazily through the last of the berries.

Tam scrambled backward, eyes wide with fear.

The bear stood up on her back legs. Her nose worked the air for the scent of the intruder. The approaching winter made the bear sluggish, but it also made her grumpy. Someone interrupting her fattening up for the winter would not be tolerated.

She caught the scent of the sheltie. She dropped to all fours and took after the dog with surprising speed.

Tam's heart crashed against his ribs as he tore across the dry grass, his hunger-starved muscles screaming. In the open meadow, the bear closed the distance. Tam felt her hot breath on his flank. He heard the click of her teeth and wet slap of her jowls as she lunged and snapped. Calling on his last bit of strength, the dog raced into the thick forest.

When his legs would no longer carry him, he squeezed as far as he could into an old hollowed tree and waited.

His breathing came in ragged gasps. His legs quivered. His nose searched for any scent of the creature.

A twig snapped.

A huge black nose sniffed the opening of the log. The bear's head blotted out the sunlight.

Tam whimpered in terror and pushed himself as far back in the log as he could.

The bear huffed and grunted. She reached one black paw into the log. Claws like curved daggers felt blindly for the dog. Tam yelped when one claw bit his forepaw. Making himself as small as he possibly could, he pushed himself against the back of the log.

The bear withdrew her paw.

Silence.

Tam's nose searched for the scent of the creature. He still smelled her, but the sound of her was gone. Tam relaxed.

Suddenly the log began to rock back and forth. Tam scrambled to keep from being thrown from his hiding place. Sick fear flooded every inch of his body. In his three years of life, he had never known fear. He had never known hunger. He had only known what every well-loved dog knows: comfort and security. This new life of constant danger was beyond his experience.

But deep within every dog is a bit of the wolf from which he descended. And that wolf gives the dog keen instinct. As the bear rocked the log harder and harder, Tam shot from the old tree like a cannonball between the bear's legs. The bear whirled and roared in frustration.

Tam raced farther into the forest and into a thick tangle of blackberry bushes. The sweet berries were long gone, but the wicked thorns remained. Tam was a small sheltie. He easily avoided the worst of the thorns by following the faint path left by foxes and skunks.

The bear reached one long arm and swiped at the wall of thorny brambles. The thorns bit deep into her skin. She jerked her furry arm back. The curved little daggers left bloody welts. The bear bawled like a baby cow. She licked at the bloody tracks on her arm. With a snort and a huff, she turned and ambled away. This creature was altogether too much trouble for her.

Tam waited and listened. He quivered both inside and out from exhaustion. He searched the breeze for the scent of the bear. The dark, evil smell was fading. Finally, he lowered his head between his paws and watched the sun move across the forest floor.

His eyes closed.

A twig snapped.

His eyes flew open. A deer.

Finally, the sun dimmed and the air cooled. Tam left the thicket and made his way back to the stream to drink. Then he retreated to the safety of the hollow tree and slept.

As Tam slept and the moon rose, a coyote hunted the

dry grass in the meadow. The smell of bear still lingered there, rank and disturbing. The coyote may have been just a few months beyond being a pup, but she knew well enough to stay away from a bear.

But there was another smell in the meadow, one the coyote could not quite read. It was not a rabbit. It was not a deer. It was certainly not a skunk or raccoon. The smell reminded her a little of the red fox who lived down in the laurel grove. And it reminded her of the warmth of the den she had shared with her mother and brothers. But not quite.

The coyote cocked her head to one side. She listened with keen concentration to faint rustling below the grass. She pounced, snatching one mouse and then another. She ate them with great satisfaction.

The coyote sat beneath the moonlight and searched the night wind for that smell she did not understand. She threw back her head and howled her questions to the moon and the mountains, then followed the thread of the unknown scent into the forest.

Tam woke stiff the next morning. With a groan, he uncurled himself and crawled out of the hollow tree. As he yawned and stretched his back legs, he sniffed the air to smell what the morning would bring. Just as he was about to shake the dirt and cobwebs from his coat, he stopped. There was a smell he had not met before. It was not deer or rabbit, nor skunk or raccoon. It was not the thick, dark smell of the bear. It was a smell somehow familiar and somehow not.

The coyote woke. She rose and stretched elaborately, first one back leg and then the other. At six months, she was all long, gangly legs and comically huge ears. She shook the night's sleep from her tan and white coat and looked around the forest. Her yellow eyes fell on Tam. The coyote stood stock-still, ears cocked forward, nose working the air.

To Tam, she looked almost like other dogs he'd met. But not quite. She had a doggish smell, except wilder. She smelled of sun and grass, blood and bones. Tam whined uncertainly and raised his tail.

The coyote did what every canine from wolf to poodle does as a sign of friendship: She wagged her tail. Her ears relaxed and she stretched her mouth in a wide coyote grin.

Fear and uncertainty of yet another wild creature Tam did not understand filled him. What was this dog that was not a dog? He raised his tail higher. A long, low growl rumbled from his chest.

The little coyote pinned her ears flat against her skull and wagged the tip of her tail in her bid for friendship.

Tam growled louder, his eyes hardening.

Then a breeze from the south whispered through the

tall pines. It made its way to Tam's nose, to his ears, *Home, home.*

Tam wheeled and set out on his course, straight and true. He crossed meadows and followed faint deer paths. The miles passed beneath his feet.

And always, always, just out of sight, followed the coyote.

CHAPTER 13

Abby

Three weeks, two days, and one hour after I lost Tam, we got a phone call.

Me and Mama had just got home from getting my cast off. Meemaw met us on the front porch, the phone held out in front of her.

"It's someone calling about Tam," she whispered.

I about fainted right there. I had prayed and prayed every night for this day, and my prayers were finally being answered.

Mama grabbed the phone. Meemaw pulled me into the house behind Mama.

"Yes, we had a dog named Tam," Mama said. "Did you find him?"

I was about to burst. Someone had found Tam! I squeezed my eyes shut. *Thank you, thank you, thank you!*

A grin split Meemaw's face. My brain galloped as fast as it could up to my room to pack Tam's things, and then down to the car and across the mountains, as fast and as far as we needed to bring Tam home.

"You found it where?" Mama asked.

I tugged at her arm. "Where is he, Mama?"

Mama shook her head and turned her back to us. "Yes, we might want it back. Could you give me your number, please? I need to talk to my husband. He's up in that area right now."

The floor felt like it was slipping under me. What was she talking about?

Mama scratched down a phone number on a piece of paper. "We'll get back in touch with you," she said, and hung up the phone.

The disappointment in her eyes told me clear as anything that my prayers had not been answered.

Meemaw gripped my shoulder. "Tell us, Holly," she said to Mama.

Mama sat on the couch. She pulled me down next to her, smoothed the hair from my face.

I pushed her hand away. "Tell me, Mama."

Mama took a shaky breath. "That was Mr. J. T. Fryar," she said. "He and his son were deer hunting a couple of days ago up near the Blue Ridge Parkway in Virginia."

I sucked in a breath. Virginia. "Was it near where we crashed?"

Mama shrugged. "He said they were by White Rock Creek and his son spotted something shiny on a tan box out in the middle of the creek. So his son waded out into the creek to see what it was."

My throat filled with a sick feeling. "What was it?" I asked.

"Tam's crate, honey," Mama said.

"And what was the shiny thing?" Meemaw asked.

Mama blinked back tears. "Tam's tags. His collar was hung up in the door of the crate."

I squeezed my eyes shut. Pictures flashed in my mind: water filling the crate, Tam clawing frantically at the crate door, him sliding into the water, his collar trapping him—

"Was there any sign of the dog?" Meemaw asked. "Any sign at all?"

I shook my head, trying to clear the terrible pictures from my head.

"No," Mama said. "He said he and his son looked around for tracks, even whistled, but . . ." Her voice trailed off.

None of us said a word when Mama finished her story. The only sound was the trees outside creaking and moaning in the wind.

Mama took my hand and squeezed it. "I'm so sorry, Abby."

I just shook my head, over and over.

"I'll call your father. He and the band just finished a gig up in Virginia. If you want, he can run up there and get the crate and Tam's collar. Do you want him to do that?"

Pure hopelessness filled every cell, every pore of my body. There was the crate and the collar, but there was no Tam.

I looked from Mama to Meemaw. Meemaw nodded just the tiniest bit.

I sighed. "I reckon so, Mama."

Two days later, Daddy pulled up in the driveway in his old VW van. In the back, surrounded by guitars and fiddles and banjos, sat Tam's crate.

Daddy and Mama stood off to the side and watched as I ran my hand over it. Mr. J. T. Fryar was right: It sure was beat-up. The sides were bashed in and claw marks made tracks in the floor of the crate. The wire door was twisted, like a giant hand had wrenched it to one side.

I turned away. I couldn't stand the thought of what it had been like for Tam.

Daddy pulled something out of his coat pocket. "I thought you'd want this," he said, handing me Tam's purple collar.

Mama slipped an arm around me and pulled me to her. "I'm sorry, Abby. I know how much you loved him."

I twisted away from her. "He might still be alive."

A look passed between Mama and Daddy.

"He could've gotten out of the crate," I said. "Just because they didn't find him, that doesn't mean—"

"Now, Abby," Daddy said, "I think it's best if you face the fact that Tam's gone. He's not coming back."

"No!" I said. I glared at both of them standing there, tears wet on their faces. I gritted my teeth. I would not cry.

"You can give up on him," I hollered. "But I won't!"

"Abby." Daddy reached out for me.

I had to get away from them and their tears and that awful, putrid crate. I tore off down the driveway, slipping and sliding on the snow and ice.

The blood pounded in my ears, saying over and over, *Tam's gone, Tam's gone.* I ran as hard as I could away from those awful words.

Finally I couldn't run anymore. I bent over, gasping for air, hugging all the pieces of me threatening to fly away. Without the hope of Tam coming home, how would I stay together?

"Abby?"

I straightened up and blinked. There stood Olivia, a bundle of bright yellow coat, little black boots, and fuzzy hat on her head. She looked for all the world like one of our baby chicks.

"What are you doing here?" I asked.

"I was about to ask you the same question," she said.

For the first time, I realized I'd run to her house.

I looked at her there, her eyes all filled up with worry and the world spinning around me a million miles an hour and my breath coming all ragged like a trapped bird trying to escape and I sat down right there in the middle of the road on the hard packed snow and said, "Tam."

"Let me think on this a minute," Olivia's granddaddy said as he built up the fire in the fireplace. "They found your little dog's crate and they found his collar. But they didn't find the dog?"

I nodded. "They said they didn't see any sign of him."

Olivia stared into the fireplace and fished the little marshmallows out of her hot chocolate with her tongue. "And you say his collar was hung up in the crate door?"

I nodded again.

"He must have slipped out of the collar, then," she said.

"That's the way I figure it too," her granddaddy said.

"So he might still be alive?" I asked.

"Well . . ." Olivia looked sideways at her granddaddy. "I can't say for sure, Abby, but logically speaking—"

"You need to talk with your meemaw," Mr. Singer said.

We both looked at him like he'd said we needed to talk with the president of the United States.

"She has the Sight," he said, nodding.

"The Sight?" Olivia asked. "What does that mean?"

A little seed of hope bloomed in my chest. "It means she can see things other folks can't." Picking up a head of steam, I said, "Meemaw and her mother and *her* mother all had the Sight. Meemaw says folks would come from all over looking for the answer to their heart's desire."

"But would that work for an animal?" Olivia asked.

I jumped up, nearly knocking my hot chocolate to the floor. "I don't know, but there's one way to find out!"

I flew out that cabin door and up the road before Olivia had time to blink.

I found Meemaw in the kitchen taking a tray of perfect-smelling cookies out of the oven.

"Why, Abby, where in the world have you been? We've been worried sick and—"

"Meemaw, I need you to do something for me."

She frowned. "What is it, darlin'?"

I took a deep breath. "I need you to use the Sight to see Tam."

Her eyes widened. Then she glanced around the kitchen. In a low voice, she said, "You know your mama don't like talk about the Sight. Besides, I don't know if it would work with a dog."

I grabbed her soft hands in mine. "Please, Meemaw.

You always said people came with questions about the people they loved the most. The things they most desired. If, for me, that's Tam, then why couldn't it work?"

She studied me for a long moment. Then she untied her apron and hung it on its hook. "Let's go up to your room."

We closed the door behind us. She shook her head. "I don't know about this," she said. "It might help if I had something of his, though."

I looked around the room. Then I remembered. "Here, Meemaw." I pulled Tam's collar out of my pocket.

She sat down in the old rocking chair Grandpa Bill made for her when Daddy was born. She closed her eyes and held Tam's collar against her chest.

I held my breath and watched her face. Snow ticked against the windowpanes.

Just when I was beginning to think it wasn't going to work, a little "Oh my!" escaped her mouth.

And like shadows slipping across our pond, alarm, fear, sadness, determination, and love flowed one to another across her face.

She pressed the collar closer. Tears slipped down her cheeks.

I couldn't help myself, I said, "Meemaw! What is it? Do you see Tam?"

Her eyes opened and found my face. Her blue, blue eyes fixed like a laser beam on me. "Abby, Tam's—"

The bedroom door opened. "Oh, Abby, here you are. I was so worried, and . . ." Mama looked from me to Meemaw and back again.

Her face went still. "What's going on in here, Agnes?"

I waved Mama away. "What did you see, Meemaw? Is Tam alive or not?"

Meemaw looked from me to Mama. She bit her lower lip, then said in almost a whisper, "Yes, Abby. I believe he is. He's trying to find his way home to you."

I yipped and about knocked Mama down, I hugged her so hard. "See, Mama! I told you! We have to leave now, Mama. We have to go find him!"

But Mama didn't look at me. Instead, she wrapped one arm around me and pulled me against her side, all the while shooting dagger eyes at Meemaw.

"Mama . . . ," I said, trying to squirm out from under her arm.

In a cold, firm voice she used on telephone salesmen, Mama said, "I don't mean any disrespect, Agnes. But I won't have you filling my daughter's head with nonsense and false hopes. She's been through enough."

"The child asked for my help, Holly," Meemaw said gently.

Meemaw and Mama stared long and hard at each other. Finally, Mama said, "Abby, I need you to take that pail of veggies out to the llamas."

I purely could not believe what I was hearing. "But *Mama . . .*"

She ran her hand over the top of my head. "Go on now, Abby. I need to talk with your grandmother."

I stormed out of the house, letting the screen door bang behind me. Which I just happen to know drives Mama crazy. "'I won't have you filling up her head with nonsense and false hope,'" I said in Mama's Ice Queen voice.

I stomped into the barn. Six long-necked, big-eared, wonderfully fuzzy llamas stopped chewing and looked at me.

"Since when is hope and believing in miracles *non-sense*?" I said. Six pairs of huge brown eyes blinked back at me. Sterling, Boo, Patches, Jet, Pearl, and Bambi shifted nervously.

I took a bunch of deep breaths to calm myself down. Llamas are a lot like shelties: They're real sensitive. And if a llama's afraid or mad, it has the unfortunate habit of spitting.

I waited for my head to clear, then offered each of the llamas carrots. Their soft, split lips scooped the goodies off my palm like velvet spoons. I stroked the wiry hair on their necks until one or two of them started to hum. Llamas hum when they feel safe and content—kind of like how a cat purrs.

I leaned my pounding head against Pearl's neck and

buried my fingers in her thick fleece. Her hum came deep and low. It worked its way through my skin and into my broken heart.

"Come home to me, Tam," I whispered. "Come home."

CHAPTER 14

Tam

Tam traveled always south, staying miles from the road. And like a gangly shadow, the coyote followed close behind.

At first it worried the dog, having this wild, unpredictable creature at his heels. She did not smell of the usual scents that mark a dog as belonging to someone: the touch of hands, foods cooked in a warm kitchen, rugs slept upon at night. This coyote smelled of leaves and wind and fresh blood.

Still, Tam watched with great curiosity as the coyote hunted the fields for mice and voles and dug the burrows of rabbits. Although there was nothing of the hunter in him, he did understand food.

At moonrise, while Tam slept, the coyote left his side. She slipped silently through the night, listening and sniffing. After she had eaten her fill, she carried a fresh kill . . . rabbit, squirrel, groundhog . . . back to Tam. She covered it with dirt and leaves and then stretched out next to him and slept.

In truth, the little coyote had been lonely when she came across Tam's scent that night. When she was five months old, a car on the Parkway had hit her mother. At first, the young coyotes stayed close to the den they had shared all their lives; eventually, though, her brothers drifted away. For weeks, she stayed close to the den and waited for her brothers to return. As the days and nights passed, her howls of calling became howls of loneliness. The night air grew crisp, and the days grew shorter. The coyote struck out from the den and all she had known.

For a time, she searched for the scents of her brothers, and called their names at night. As days turned to weeks, she lost the specific memory of her family. She knew only that she was alone, and the desire not to be alone drove her.

In this way, she followed Tam along the narrow deer trails, day after day, always heading south. It didn't matter to her which direction they traveled, as long as they were together. Oh, there was still the puppy in the coyote. Often she would circle wide around Tam, just out of sight, and wait hidden from him. As Tam passed, the coyote pounced from behind tree or bush. When Tam stopped to rest, she nipped and bowed in an invitation to play. Tam rebuffed her every time. He was a dog on his way home.

Tam and the coyote worked their way steadily south, descending into the flats of the Otter Creek drainage. The hunting was good, the weather cool and fine. Tam felt stronger than he had since the accident.

After crisscrossing Otter Creek for several miles, they arrived at the banks of the James River. This was no narrow, tumbling creek. Tam had grown used to crossing those. The James River was wide and slow. And deep. Tam had never seen anything like it.

The coyote trotted along the riverbank, investigating odd pieces of garbage. She rolled with delight on a dead fish. She stood, shook herself, and trotted back over to Tam, nipping him playfully on the ear.

Tam growled the annoying creature away. He did not feel like playing. The way south, the way he must go, was across the river, and Tam saw no way to cross. He'd grown accustomed to hopping stone by stone across smaller creeks and streams or crossing a fallen tree. But this river was far too wide for even the tallest hemlock to span.

After an hour of searching for a place to cross, Tam collapsed in the shade, tired and disappointed. He sighed and watched, brown eyes full of misery, as the river lumbered past. A hawk circled lazily above a small spit of land in the middle of the river; a squirrel chattered in the branches above Tam. The coyote stretched out beside her friend as close as she dared and closed her eyes.

And three miles to the west, a raven called from the top of the James River Bridge, arching easily across the river.

Late afternoon. Tam rose. The need to go south was stronger than ever. He whined. It was time, time to see his girl. Time to hear her call, "Tam! Come on, Tam!"

The coyote woke and followed the dog's gaze across the river. She shook herself and then waded into the water.

The coyote was a natural, fearless swimmer. Her mother had taught her and her brothers early and well. She paddled easily in the deep water, back high, tail streaming behind like a rudder. She scrabbled back up to shore and called to Tam.

Tam whined and took one tentative step toward the river. He raised his nose to the wind. Surely the coyote was wrong. Surely there must be another way to cross.

The coyote called to him again and then waded out in the river. She swam out and circled back.

Tam took two steps closer to the water's edge, whimpering. There is no more pitiful a thing in this wide world than a dog torn between what he needs and what he fears.

The coyote struck out for a small spit of land in the middle of the river.

Whining, crouching to a belly crawl, Tam crept into the water.

Tam was not a natural swimmer. His back and hips sank below the surface. He strained to keep his head above the swirl and slap of water. His long, thick coat billowed around him. Still, it was not as bad as he'd feared.

Until the current caught him.

Tam thrashed with all his might to keep his head just above the surface. His front paws beat against the current. He cried out. Where were the rescuing arms of his girl? Where was his safe home?

The coyote had just pulled herself onto the shore of the small island when she heard Tam's cry. The coyote sat on the shore, head cocked to one side. Why was her friend not coming to the island? The coyote yipped. Perhaps he didn't see her.

The current quickened. The placid river became a turbulent concoction of water and rocks. The current caught Tam like a piece of discarded paper, swirling and plunging his body downstream. Water rushed up his nose, bringing back a flood of memories from that day weeks and many miles ago. Again and again, the roiling water grabbed him in a fierce hold, dashing him against rocks and boulders. But no matter how the river tried to deceive him, Tam stayed true to his southern journey.

His shoulder clipped a rock, spinning him downward. Water filled his lungs. Grayness closed over him. He could no longer tell the murky river depths from the sky. His legs became heavy, all but useless.

The coyote watched with growing alarm as the current swept Tam away from the island. She raced along the shore, trying to keep her friend in sight. Tam's head disappeared beneath the water. She yipped and called to her friend. She launched herself and struck out for the fast-moving current.

A feeling of utter hopelessness gripped the dog. He was tired, so very tired. He no longer knew the way home.

Then he remembered, almost as if the girl were nearby, calling to him: "Tam! Come here, Tam!" The sheltie drove his forelegs with more strength than he ever imagined having. Somewhere, his girl was calling and he must go to her.

As Tam's head broke the surface he was aware of two things: air and the coyote.

The coyote paddled hard against Tam, turning him upstream. She knew how to angle her body toward the calm water close to shore. She and her brothers had made a game of it in the long, hot days of summer.

Calling on all her skill and strength, she used her body to brace Tam and steered them slowly to shore. Just as she felt she could swim no farther, the current calmed to stillness. Their paws touched the sandy bottom. They had made it across, together.

Tam had barely the strength to pull himself clear of the water's edge. His small body was battered and bruised. The weight of the water in his coat was almost too much to bear. He staggered, then dragged himself to a patch of dying sunlight. He vomited water and then collapsed.

The coyote whined and pawed at her friend. She licked the side of his mouth, something she knew he hated. Even his growling and snapping was better than this. But Tam didn't move. He didn't open his eyes.

When the last of the afternoon sun slipped behind the ridge, a sharp wind arose. Tam trembled in the cold.

With a whimper and a sigh, the coyote coiled her body around his. She did not move when tempting mice rustled in the dry grass along the riverbank. Her ears barely twitched when a fox, then a deer, came down to the water to drink. When cold wind blew across the high mountains all the way from Canada, she wrapped her body tighter around her friend, her true heart beating in time with his.

CHAPTER 15

Abby

"Okay, here's another one," Olivia said, squinting at the computer screen. "It's called Fairhope County Shelter. It's not all that close to where you lost Tam, but he may have wandered farther by now, so I'll print it out."

"Thanks, Olivia," I said. I squeezed closer to her at the school library's computer station. "That gives me six to start calling, now that the ranger station is closed for the winter."

I'd discovered that the other day when I made my daily phone call. I about died. It was my friend Olivia, the smartest kid in all of Harmony Gap, who came up with the idea of calling animal shelters.

The bell rang. Olivia logged off the computer. "We'll

just work our way south and find more to call."

"Like Tam," I said.

Olivia took off her glasses and began to clean them carefully, always a sure sign she was thinking of how best to say something hard. I braced myself.

"Abby, I don't want you to get your hopes up too high. I know how much you and Tam loved each other, and he was one smart dog."

"Don't talk about him like he's dead," I snapped.

She sighed and put her glasses back on. "All I'm saying is be careful, Abby."

I slung my pack on my back and stomped off to music class without a backward glance.

Two nights later, Daddy came up to my room. He picked up my guitar and sat down in the window seat. He strummed the opening notes to "The Water Is Wide," one of our favorites to sing together.

"Your mama tells me you're calling animal shelters all over Virginia. Says you're going to put us in the poorhouse with all those calls."

Not looking up from the map I was working on, I said, "It's only six shelters, not that many. And I don't call each and every one of them every single day."

Daddy set the guitar aside and came to sit on my bed. "Money's tight right now, peanut. And Christmas is just around the corner."

I just shrugged. I drew Mr. J. T. Fryar's son finding Tam's crate and collar in White Rock Creek onto my map.

"Which is why," Daddy continued, "I'm leaving again, right after Thanksgiving."

"I heard," I muttered.

"From who?"

I sighed and set my sketch pad aside. "From you and Mama," I said. "I could hear y'all fighting about it this morning. Mama sounded pretty mad."

It was Daddy's turn to sigh. "Yeah, I'm in the doghouse with your mama. As usual."

"You'll be back in time for Christmas, won't you?"

Daddy smiled. "Wouldn't miss it for anything, sugar."

I studied my daddy's face for a long time. His eyes were still the bluest blue, his nose straight and strong. He had Meemaw's red hair, wild as an Appalachian storm in the summertime. I knew exactly how he smelled.

"I wish I could go with you, Daddy," I said. "Be your navigator."

Daddy grinned. "You came by loving maps rightly. Your mama and me driving all over the place, you just a tiny little baby sitting in her lap, looking at the map. Your mama always swore you liked having her make up bedtime stories straight from the lines on the road atlas."

"I wish too you *wouldn't* go," I confessed.

"I got to follow my north star, Abby honey. Being a professional musician is my dream."

"Just like the three wise men followed that north star to Bethlehem?" I said.

"Just like." Daddy nodded like he was agreeing with himself. "Most folks got a north star in their life—something that gives their life extra meaning. Mine is music."

Without even thinking, I said, "Mine is Tam."

Mama says to her mind, Thanksgiving is the best holiday ever. She says it's all about family and friends and good food to share. "Thanksgiving is all about *sharing*," Mama said as we peeled apples for the pies. "Not about *getting*."

I was thinking about that as I looked around the table. Mama sat next to Daddy with shining eyes. I knew they were holding hands under the table. Olivia and her granddaddy sat across from me, Mr. Singer saying for the millionth time to Meemaw, "I ain't never eaten so much good food in my life."

Meemaw laughed. "You ate that turkey and dressing like a man with a hollow leg, Alphus."

Daddy winked at me. "Do turkeys still come with wishbones, peanut?"

Meemaw jumped up and took something off the top of the woodstove. "Just had it over there drying," she said, handing a big ol' wishbone to Daddy.

Daddy narrowed his eyes and studied the two prongs. "Looks perfect for wishing on to me. What do you think, Miss Olivia? Abby?"

We both grinned and nodded.

We each took hold of one piece of the bone. "Make your wishes, girls," Mama said.

I closed my eyes and pictured Tam grinning at me with his rich brown eyes. I felt his head on my knee.

"You ready?" Daddy asked. We both nodded.

"Okay," he said. "One, two, three . . ."

Snap!

"Well for pity's sake, would you look at that?" Meemaw exclaimed.

I opened my eyes and looked at the bones we held. They were exactly the same length!

Olivia shook her head. "I don't think I've ever seen that before."

"You must have each had awful powerful wishes," Olivia's granddaddy said, scratching his beard.

I wanted so bad to ask Olivia what she'd wished for. But Daddy said, "I'm not a smart enough man to know what that means, but I do know it's high time for some music."

"Mama," he said to Meemaw, "go and grab that old autoharp of yours. Abby, get your guitar."

"I'll get my banjo tuned up," Mr. Singer said.

Daddy swatted Mama on the behind. "And you go park your sweet self at the piano, my lovely Holly Prescott Whistler. It's long past time we had some music in our house."

We all hurried to do what Daddy'd said. We tuned and argued about what song to play. Daddy put the fiddle under his chin and struck the first sweet notes of "The Wind That Shakes the Barley" and we all got swept away. Then he swung right into a fast version of "Rocky Top." We about got dizzy trying to keep up. Olivia sang at the top of her lungs. We all laughed so hard, we didn't even hear the wind and sleet slapping the house. I decided right then and there that Thanksgiving beat Christmas hands down.

I took my fingers off my guitar strings to give them a rest. Purely out of habit, my hand dropped to the side of my chair to scratch Tam's ears. But there was no soft fur, no tongue licking the tips of my fingers. Only sad emptiness sat beside my chair.

Two weeks, six days, and eight minutes after Daddy left for his tour, he called.

"Hey, peanut!" he boomed over the phone. "How's the best girl in all of Harmony Gap doing?"

"Pretty good," I said. "I got a test tomorrow in civics,

Daddy. Why in the world are they giving us a test on the last day before Christmas break I will never understand."

"Does seem kind of crazy to me too," he said with a laugh. "Maybe Olivia will let you cheat off her paper."

I laughed too and burrowed deeper into the blanket on the couch. "Olivia would never do that, and you know it."

"Well, I'll be home by this time tomorrow night."

"Really, Daddy?"

"Really and truly, darlin'. And I'm coming home with some big news."

"Tell me," I said. For just a minute, I wondered if he knew something about Tam.

I heard somebody telling him to hurry up.

"I got to go, Abby. I'll tell everybody tomorrow night."

"But Daddy . . ."

"Sleep tight, sugar. Tell your mama and Meemaw I'm coming home tomorrow."

I held the phone to my chest. Mama came from the barn all covered with snow.

"Daddy just called," I said.

"Humph . . ." she grumbled, pulling off her boots and shaking snow from her coat.

"Says he'll be home by this time tomorrow night and he's got big news," I said.

Mama came over and plopped down on the end of the couch. She pulled my feet into her lap and started rubbing them. Her hands were cold, but I didn't mind.

"What do you think that news could be, Mama?"

"I hope it's that he won the lottery." Mama laughed. But it was a tired kind of laugh.

I nudged Mama with my foot. "What would you buy with a million dollars?"

This was a game me and Mama played when we were driving in the car. Sometimes we named serious things like food for all the starving animals in the world. But most of the time, it was just plain silly stuff like our own Ferris wheel or the world's biggest, fanciest popcorn maker like in the movie theater.

This time, though, Mama just stared up at the ceiling and said, "Peace of mind."

CHAPTER 16

Tam

The last days of fall gave way to cold rain and sleet. After a wet, miserable day of travel, the dog and the coyote found the remains of an old wooden shed in a clearing. They hid in the thick laurel, watching and listening for signs of humans. Satisfied they were safe, they slipped under a split-rail fence and into the dry, dark shed. The air smelled of rotten hay and corn. Rusted farm tools and tattered feed sacks lay scattered in the far corner. Rain tapped on the tin roof.

Tam heard scurrying from under the feed bags. Without thinking, he pounced and grabbed. His mouth filled with fur and warm, fresh blood. Tam dropped the rat as if it were a hot coal, took a step back, and whined.

He pawed at the rat. Why didn't it move? The smell of blood made Tam's mouth water. He licked at the bloody body, growing hungrier.

The coyote snatched up the rat, the tail hanging out one side of her mouth, the head out the other. Tam growled, flashing his teeth. The rat was his. Despite the fact that she had fed him all these weeks; despite the fact that she could maim him with one slash to the throat, the young coyote dropped the rat, trotted to the corner of the shed, and watched as Tam ate his first kill.

That night, as rain changed to sleet and sleet to snow, as the approaching winter beat back the remnants of fall, as Tam and the coyote slept pressed against each other amid the remains of the rat, blood speckling the white ruff around Tam's chest, the old Tam slipped away. Away went the Tam who slept in a warm bed, who had his food served to him in a dish. All that remained of that Tam was the girl: the sound of her voice, the feel of her hands, her smell. And the drive to go south.

For two days wind howled and pushed against the shed as the temperatures dropped. Tam and the coyote slept close together for warmth, only leaving the shed to relieve themselves or drink from a nearby stream. The rats that had made the shed their home had scattered.

On the third morning, Tam was awakened by the

sound of a wet *whump*. For the first time in days, a shaft of sunlight streamed through the doorway. Tam rose, arched his back, and yawned. He looked to his side for the sleeping coyote. She was gone. Tam sniffed the old feed sack the coyote slept on and followed her scent to the doorway.

White, white snow blanketed the meadow, sparkling in the morning sun. Above, a raven cawed, landing on the branch of a tall spruce and sending the snow to the ground with a loud *whump*. The coyote's tracks cut the smooth blanket from the doorway to the split-rail fence on the edge of the meadow.

Tam followed her tracks, lifting each paw distastefully. It may have been white, and it may have been frozen, but it was still water.

Just as Tam was halfway across the meadow, he heard a yip and saw, from the corner of his eye, a brown blur barreling toward him. The thing knocked him on his side and rolled him onto his back. He tried to scramble to his feet, but the wet, heavy snow held him fast. He was stuck, belly exposed.

Above Tam, grinning wide, tongue lolling out one side of her mouth, was the coyote. She nipped at his forelegs waving uselessly in the air, then nipped at his back legs.

She pounced at his head and pulled hard at the white ruff around his neck. Tam snapped at her, tried to right himself, but it was no use. Every time he almost got his feet under him, she knocked him over again. Tam was furious.

Finally, Tam's claws found purchase in the ground beneath the snow. He scrambled to his feet and knocked the coyote to one side with his broad chest. He whirled, grabbing the coyote's back leg. She yelped, nipped his ear, and took off across the meadow.

Tam tore after her. They leaped over the split-rail fence. They shot around snow-laden laurel thickets and moss-covered boulders. The coyote lost her footing. Tam grabbed the end of her tail and pulled. The coyote whipped around and grabbed the side of Tam's face. They tumbled down an icy bank in a tangle of fur. They broke through the laced ice on the edge of the creek, into the cold water.

The two pulled themselves up onto the bank, shook the water from their coats, and panted happily. The coyote licked a small, bleeding wound on the side of Tam's face. Tam's tail waved back and forth. He couldn't stay mad at the little coyote.

They drank side by side from the stream, then followed the scent of a rabbit back up to the fence. They found the rabbit's den beneath the crumbled remains of a stone chimney. Together they dug beneath the snow where the earth was still warm. Tam flushed the frightened rabbit. The coyote caught it in two bounds, snapped its neck, and carried it back to Tam.

* * *

Three days after it appeared, the snow was gone. The tree branches once again stretched toward the sky; rhododendron and mountain laurel thickets regained their fullness. Squirrels, rabbits, and chipmunks busied themselves gathering the last of their winter food. Birds filled the trees. This first snow of the high country was gone, leaving behind a sense of urgency.

Tam awakened that morning with the need to continue south. Leaving the warm shelter of the shed, he and the coyote slipped under the fence and crossed the creek.

As they descended into the Roanoke Valley, the thick forests gave way to hay fields, rolling farmland, and the occasional homestead. By late afternoon, they found themselves in an old apple orchard, long abandoned.

Tam chewed a shriveled wild green apple and watched the coyote on the edge of the orchard. She turned her head to one side, cocking an ear. Her body tensed. Almost imperceptibly, she lowered her haunches, arched her back. From a dead standstill, she sprang straight up into the air, arcing over the tall grass. Two more pounces in quick succession and she emerged with a large field rat hanging limply from her jaws. Tam trotted over and wagged his tail hopefully. But she did not share her meal this time. This was her kill. Tam would have to make his own.

Tam scouted the tall grass too. The orchard, with its

rotting apples, was a haven for field rats and meadow voles. Although Tam could not match the coyote's pouncing technique, he was fast and agile. By nightfall, he too had a full belly.

That night, as he and his friend lay together beneath a rocky outcropping, stars glittered like ice in the night sky. The next morning, a hard frost coated the ground and studded the grass. Winter followed close at their heels.

CHAPTER 17

Abby

I sat in my window seat, my sketch pad in my lap and an atlas by my side. From up here in my bedroom window seat, I could see all of the front yard, the smaller barn off to the side, and all the way down to the road where Daddy'd be driving up anytime now.

I rubbed by thumb back and forth over Tam's collar while I studied the map of the Blue Ridge Parkway in the atlas.

See, Olivia had had this idea:

I'd gone down to her house to apologize for biting her head off at school the other day when she'd told me not to set my hopes too high on finding Tam.

"I just can't give up on him, Olivia," I'd said. "I don't

know how to be Abby without Tam. Does that make a bit of sense?"

She'd smiled that sad smile she carries around most of the time and nodded. We sat there in her prancing-unicorn-princess room (which she told me she hates, but she loves her grandaddy too much to say), listening to the wind. Finally, she'd said, "Abby, do you think *you* might have the Sight, just like your grandmother?"

I frowned. "I don't think so. She sees into the future and stuff."

"Yes, but doesn't it run in her family? Didn't you say her mother and her grandmother had the Sight?"

"Well, sure, but . . ." It had just never occurred to me before.

"It may be different for different people," she said. "And you've told me about these dreams and stuff you've had about Tam. Maybe that's how it works for you. Try putting what you've seen into one of those maps of yours. And trust your instincts."

So that's what I was trying to do. I'd made a list of all the things I could remember from the dreams and visions I'd had of Tam—the kinds of trees, what the mountains looked like, rivers, creeks, and such. I'd look at the atlas, then draw a while, then look at the Blue Ridge map some more. At first it was like trying to fit together the first few pieces of a giant jigsaw puzzle. Nothing seemed to make sense or go together. But the more I worked at it, it did. It did start to make sense. Tam was trying to find his way home. I knew it sure as anything.

That night, we all sat around the dining room table looking at Daddy. Ever since he'd walked in the door, he looked like he was about to bust. He was lit up like a Christmas tree.

Mama blew out a long breath. "Okay, Ian. Enough suspense. What's this big news?"

Daddy stood and pulled something from his back pocket. He gave me a wink.

My heart jumped up my throat. Tam! My maps were right!

He unfolded the paper and held it out for all to see.

Meemaw squinted at the tiny print. "What in the world is it, son?"

Mama leaned so far across the table to get a look at that paper, her hair dragged in her mashed potatoes.

Her mouth dropped open. Her eyes went wide as hubcaps. "Good lord, Ian. Is that what I think it is?"

"Yes, ma'am, my beautiful Holly Prescott Whistler. It's a recording contract! Nashville wants the Clear Creek Boys!"

Mama jumped up from her chair and ran over to Daddy. They grabbed each other and danced around like a couple of crazy people.

Meemaw and I just sat there watching them, dumbfounded.

Daddy scooped Mama up in his arms and twirled her around and around. Mama laughed and laughed. I did too.

"We are Nashville bound!" Daddy whooped.

"When?" Mama asked.

"They want us there by January fifth," Daddy said. "I figure we'll try and get there no later than the first. That'll give us time to get Abby settled into a new school and—"

"Wait . . . what?" I gasped. "What do you mean, a new school?"

Daddy looked at me like I was an idiot. Mama studied her shoes.

"I think, Abby honey, your daddy means y'all are moving to Nashville," Meemaw whispered.

I looked from Meemaw to Mama to Daddy, shaking my head. "No, Daddy. I can't. I can't go."

Daddy pulled on the end of his nose. "Of course you'll go, peanut. We're a family and . . ."

"No, Daddy!" I was shaking all over. "Tam's on his way home! I have to be here for him!"

"Now, Abby," Daddy frowned. "It's been almost three months. He's gone, honey. It's time to let go."

I jumped up so quick, my chair fell over backward.

"He's alive, Daddy! I can feel it! I been working real hard on my maps, and . . . and Meemaw saw him!"

Mama shot Meemaw a look. Daddy looked like he wanted to be anywhere but in our dining room.

I looked at the three of them all looking at me, my mouth opening and closing like a landlocked fish.

Daddy took a step toward me, holding out his hand. "Come on, Abby," he said.

I slapped my napkin into my dinner plate, scattering peas every which way. "I. Won't. Go. To. Nashville!" Then I bolted for my room.

CHAPTER 18

Tam

Tam's feet twitched in his sleep, a desperate *woof* slipping from his throat. The coyote cracked one eye open, then slipped back to shallow sleep.

Tam rarely dreamed now about the girl or his home with her. Most times, his dreams were filled with chasing, or being chased. Bit by bit, Tam was forgetting his life before: before the car crash, the swirling creek, before the coyote, the snap of bone, the taste of fresh blood. Although Tam had traveled well over a hundred and thirty miles since he'd last been someone's dog, the real distance was inside him.

He still felt driven to go south. But like the coyote, he didn't question the why of it; he just went where instinct led him. If the coyote had decided she no longer wanted to go south, or that it was best to head east or to stay put for the winter, Tam would have done that. Home, now, was being with her.

It snowed hard for two days. Mid-December winds blew drifts of snow so deep, Tam had a difficult time shouldering his way through. He used precious energy just to make one or two miles. Hunting was difficult. Any extra weight Tam had put on during the Indian summer was melting away.

The coyote was built for snow. Her wide paws splayed on the surface like snowshoes, allowing her to travel easily. Her narrow chest knifed through the deeper drifts. But like Tam, hunting proved difficult for her too. She and Tam had little fat to keep them warm as they slept beneath the low, deep boughs of a hemlock. They awoke hungry and went to sleep hungry.

After several days, the two lay in the sun on a rock ledge overlooking a meadow. The snow had finally stopped.

Tam closed his eyes against the glare of the sun on snow. His head tipped forward as he dozed.

Suddenly the coyote tensed beside him. Tam opened his eyes and followed her gaze down to the edge of the trees on the far side of the meadow. There, a gray form ambled across the snow. Tam lifted his muzzle, catching the scent. It was not a scent he had met before. As he was about to lay his head down on his paws, the coyote slipped off the ledge, eyes fixed on the lumbering animal below.

She moved with fluid silence. Keeping low and downwind, she swung to the left, skirting the edge of the forest. Tam sat up and watched with interest as she slipped up behind the creature. Tam expected her to arc high in the air and pounce, as she always did.

Instead, the coyote barked. Tam jumped off the ledge and pushed his way through the snow. A chase would soon be on and the coyote would need him.

The creature turned to face the coyote. Sun lit the black tips of the long, needlelike quills bristling from every inch of its body.

The coyote darted forward, snapping at the face of the porcupine, the only part of its body not protected by quills. She and her brothers had learned the hard way about the sharp, stinging quills. They had also learned how sweet the meat of the tender belly of the porcupine is. The trick was to either crush the head in one snap or flip the porcupine over, exposing the unprotected belly.

Tam barked his way down to the coyote and the porcupine.

The porcupine swung her head to the side to see Tam.

The coyote rushed in, snapping at the creature's nose.

The porcupine swung her tail. Quills raked the side of the coyote's neck. She dodged most of them. One or two lodged harmlessly in the thick rough around her neck. She licked her lips, tasting the porcupine's blood.

Tam darted forward. He snapped at the porcupine's side. He yelped and tumbled back, shaking his head. His face was full of quills.

Tam's attack was just enough distraction for the coyote. She rushed in, shoved her long muzzle beneath the porcupine, and flipped her onto her back. The quills stuck fast in the snow, pinning the porcupine to the ground. The coyote tore at the exposed throat, the belly.

In seconds, it was over.

Tam wiped furiously at the stinging barbs in his face. One pierced the tender side of his black nose. Several more hung from his chin and the side of his mouth. One had barely missed an eye. He managed to dislodge most of the quills by scrubbing his face with his paws. He rubbed his face in the wet snow to cool the terrible burning.

The coyote tore open the underside of the dead porcupine. Tam wagged his tail. In her hunger, the coyote forgot herself and bared her teeth. Then, just as quickly, she pinned her ears back in apology, wagging her tail low.

Tam had never tasted meat so warm and so sweet. He forgot the pain in his face. He ate until his shrunken belly could hold no more. They stripped the carcass clean.

Later, when raven, then badger, then bobcat checked the carcass for any remaining meat or bones, they would find nothing on the snow but blood and quills.

That night, their bellies were full. Warm inside the remains of an abandoned mill, the coyote worked all but one of the quills from Tam's face with her tongue.

For several days, Tam and the coyote made their way along faint logging roads. Wilderness yielded to small family farms, spread like patchwork quilts across the landscape. The orchards, gardens, and wood lots brought flashes of memory back to Tam again: deer browsing an orchard; an old woman talking as she bent among the plants in her garden. The memories filled Tam's heart with a longing he could not name, pulling him toward the houses below.

But the coyote was afraid. Something deep within her was frightened by the scent of people. As Tam coursed down the hill toward the farmstead beyond, the coyote called to him from the edge of the trees.

A girl's voice drifted up from inside the house. Tam hesitated. There had been another girl once, hadn't there? Tam whined and took another step away from the coyote and toward the house.

The coyote took one step, then another, away from the safety of the trees. Every nerve in her body told her to retreat, to hide. How could she follow? How could she not?

Tam stopped and looked over his shoulder at his friend. He barked once for her to come.

But as much as the coyote loved Tam, she could not follow. She sat down, threw her muzzle to the fading sky, and howled her misery.

A screen door slammed in the house below. The sharp sound carried like gunshot. The coyote whirled and dashed for the forest.

For a split second, Tam's heart divided between the longing to be with his friend and the shadow of a girl.

The coyote yipped from the woods. Without a backward glance, Tam turned and joined the coyote in the cover of the forest.

CHAPTER 19

Abby

If I was to draw a map of that Christmas, it would look like this: rivers overflowing with unshed tears; bare, heartbroken trees without a single apple; no deer, no birds, and no songs. And one single, solitary house without a Christmas tree.

Well, that's not exactly right, I reckon. We did get a Christmas tree. Sort of. Before, Daddy and I would go way back in the forest on our land and cut our own. We made a real big deal of it too. And Tam was always right there with us, supervising the whole thing.

But this year the big deal was moving. No time to spend the better part of the day wandering and singing, looking for just the right tree. Instead, we went into town, just like everybody else, and got a store-bought tree.

As for that map, I couldn't have drawn it anyway, even if I'd wanted to. I was too wore out. Wore out from doing my level best to convince Mama and Daddy to let me stay behind with Meemaw. Wore out from trying to convince Meemaw to convince Mama and Daddy that she *needed* me to stay behind.

Remembering what Miss Peasly had said, I told her, "Meemaw, you can't handle this place all by yourself. It's too much for a woman alone. That's why we came to live in your house in the first place."

"I appreciate your concern, child," Meemaw said. "But *your* place is with your mama and daddy. I'll be just fine."

Finally, I was purely worn out from saying too many good-byes.

I said good-bye to my teacher, Mrs. Radley, and Principal Atticus when Mama and I went to pick up my school records. "I'll miss you, Abby," Mrs. Radley said. "You kept things interesting around here."

I said good-bye to Miss Eugenia Quatch, the librarian at the Balsam County Library, when I returned my library books. She smiled from behind her big wooden desk. "We had many spirited discussions about books, didn't we?"

"Yes, ma'am, we sure did."

"You tell Olivia to keep me informed of all your doings in the big city. And promise you'll stop in and see me when you're back in town?"

I swallowed hard. "Yes, ma'am, I promise."

I said good-bye to each and every apple tree and thanked them for their goodness. I crept beneath the curtain of branches of the big willow tree on the banks of Clear Creek. "You always provided a cool, secret place for me and Tam in the summer." The long, dry limbs rustled in reply. I looked up into the gnarled branches and said, "I surely do appreciate you letting me climb all over you and for not pitching me out onto the ground."

I said good-bye to Clear Creek and to our little pond, Lake Inferior, and to the front porch and the tire swing Daddy'd hung for me in the old oak tree when we first moved here.

In the days before we left, Mama spent a lot of time in the barn with the llamas. Even though she knew that between Meemaw and Olivia and Olivia's granddaddy they'd get more attention than they could stand, she still came into the house wiping at her eyes. She said it was from the cold, but I suspect she was saying her good-byes too. Mama loved those llamas more than anything.

Olivia didn't have a lot of patience for good-byes.

"For heaven's sake, Abby," she said, when I complained for the millionth time that Mama and Daddy were unreasonable. "Of course you have to go with them."

"But Olivia, you know why I have to stay here! What

if Tam comes back and—"

"And what if he doesn't?" she snapped. My mouth fell open. I'd never, ever heard Olivia use a harsh voice before.

She took off her glasses and wiped them on the bottom of her shirt. In a voice I could barely make out, she said, "At least you have parents. I'd follow mine to the ends of the earth if they were still alive."

At that moment, I felt about as low as a bug's butt.

The night before we were to set out for Nashville, Olivia handed me an envelope. "What's this?" I asked.

She smiled. "I'm not good at good-byes," she said. "Read it later."

I threw my arms around her and hugged her little self to me. "I'm going to miss you," I said. "You won't forget me, will you?"

"Oh, Abby," Olivia said, "don't be so dramatic. Grandfather and I will be up here a bunch to help your grandmother with the llamas. Every square inch of this place will remind me of you. Besides," she said, "this will force you to get email and join the twenty-first century."

The next morning, when Mama and I pulled out of our driveway, that little trailer hitched to Mama's truck bumping along behind; when I looked back and saw Meemaw growing smaller and smaller as she waved from the front porch, the wind and snow swirling around her, my body still feeling her hugging me, I remembered a map from my world history book. It was an old, old map from the ancient explorer days. It was a map of the world as they knew it, with countries and rivers and towns. But beyond what they knew was a big blank space with nothing but the words *Terra Incognita, Unknown Territory*.

That's exactly how I felt that day as we left my home in the mountains.

CHAPTER 20

Tam

Tam and the coyote made good distance following the deer trails meandering along the shoulder of the mountains below the ridge. Although it was rarely above freezing, and the late December nights bitter, the snow was solid, making for easy travel.

Still, food was scarce. They caught the occasional squirrel and mouse. The coyote crunched old acorns and dried-up berries. But they'd not had full bellies since the porcupine.

And although the porcupine had filled Tam's belly with sweet, rich meat, it had also left one side of his face swollen and painful. The one quill the coyote was unable to lick free had worked its way deep into Tam's cheek. As December drew to a close, the swelling and fever increased.

Tam and the coyote traveled slowly through new snow on a deer trail. Tam was weak and tired from hunger and fever. The coyote stayed beside him until he stopped to rest or sleep, then she'd go in search of food. By evening, they'd only covered six miles.

They entered a small, moonlit clearing. Both Tam and the coyote smelled food. Something delicious lay buried beneath the snow and pine branches.

The coyote reached the spot first. She reached a paw out to scratch away a pine branch.

Snap!

The coyote yowled. She jumped and twisted straight into the air. The snow and branches scattered, revealing the awful truth: the metal jaws of a trap held the coyote's foot fast.

Tam flattened his ears in fear. He stretched his neck forward and sniffed the evil trap. Bright red blood spattered the snow, pooling under the coyote's foot. She looked at Tam, eyes wide with fright, and cried pitifully.

Despite his painful face, Tam barked and snapped at the trap. He dug frantically where the metal chain disappeared beneath the ground. It was no use. There was nothing Tam could do to help his friend. He lay down beside her, licked the side of her face and the trapped paw. As the moon traced across the winter sky, a great horned owl hunted not far away, and deer huddled together for warmth in the long grass. Tam wrapped his body tight around the shivering coyote.

Sunlight found the clearing the next morning, warming the backs of coyote and dog. Tam woke. He stood and sniffed the coyote. She smelled of blood and fear and sickness. She lay on her side, whimpered once to Tam, and thumped her tail at him.

Tam stood protectively above her. He stooped now and then to lick her grotesquely swollen foot or to whine consolation to her. A thick, low fog crept into the clearing.

Fever in his face drove him away from his friend's side down to a small stream in search of water. He drank so intently to cool the heat in his body, he did not hear or smell the man until it was too late.

A shot rang out. Tam froze. A sharp, acrid smell filled the air. Tam crept up the bank and through the rhododendron forest on the edge of the clearing where the coyote was.

The sight that greeted him filled him with fear. A tall human stood over the little coyote. He kicked at her with the toe of his boot. Tam expected her to snap at the human or at least cry out. But she was silent.

The human kneeled down beside her, pulled the jaws of the steel trap apart, freeing her foot.

Tam tensed, readying himself. Surely now, she would run and they could be away from this terrible place.

But the coyote didn't move.

The human held the coyote's limp body up by the tail. Tam whined. The coyote's eyes, the eyes that had looked at him so many times in joy and concern, were empty. The strong, lithe body that had warmed his, that had covered more than a hundred miles beside him, hung lifeless.

Tam's heart broke. He threw back his head and howled his pain for his friend.

"What the—" The human whirled. He dropped the coyote to the ground, squinting into the swirling fog. He grabbed his gun, aimed at the rhododendron, and fired.

The blast of the shotgun boomed in Tam's ears. In a panic, he darted out into the clearing. Between him and the far side of the clearing was the body of the coyote, the trap, and the human with the gun. Tam crouched and looked side to side for some way to escape.

"Well, looky here," the human said, grinning. "It's a New Year's Day two-for-one special: a coyote and a fox." The human raised the long black barrel of the shotgun. Tam pulled back his lips and snarled, taking one step toward his friend. She had saved his life more times than he could remember. How could he leave her now?

Tam rushed the human, slashing his leg as he streaked past.

The human cried out in surprise and pain. "A dog! Must be rabid."

With helpless rage, Tam stood over the body of the coyote, hackles raised, teeth bared. A low growl rumbled from his chest. His hard eyes, filled with pure hate, fixed on the human.

The man raised his shotgun to his shoulder and squinted at Tam. "Only one thing for a rabid dog."

The world exploded. The blast lifted Tam off the ground and tumbled him backward. Pain unlike anything he had ever felt shot through his shoulder.

Footsteps stomped through the dead leaves and snow. Tam scrambled to his feet and tried to run. His front left leg refused to move. It hung limply and painfully at his side.

Another shot rang out above his head. "Come back here, you devil dog!"

Tam ran through the forest as fast as his three legs could take him. Blood streamed from the wound.

Footsteps quickened behind him, coming closer.

Tam lost his footing. He slid down a mud-frozen bank to the creek. The human tripped and slid, cursing.

A skin of ice covered the creek. Slick, black rocks jutted through the frozen surface like rotten teeth. Tam knew if he could get across, he could lose the human in the twisted laurel and rhododendron. Tam stepped carefully onto the ice. Water gurgled beneath.

The human stood on the bank at the edge of the ice. He raised his gun. "Say your prayers."

Tam dodged to the side. The bullet whined past his ear. He scrambled blindly toward the far bank, away from the human and the gun and the sad, empty body of the coyote.

The ice cracked beneath Tam's feet. Before he could save himself, he plunged into the freezing water and was carried away.

WINTER

CHAPTER 21

Abby

"You sure you don't want me to come with you?" Mama asked.

From the safety of the school office, I watched all the kids at Jesse Rogers Middle School stream through the front doors. I had never in all my life seen so many kids, so many different kinds of kids, in one place.

It was January 4, my first day at a new school. My mouth felt dry as crackers.

Before I could work up enough spit to get an answer out, a tall lady with curly ginger hair walked in the office. She smiled at me and Mama.

"You must be our new student, Abigail Whistler," she said.

"Abby," Mama corrected. "She goes by Abby."

The lady smiled right into my eyes. "Is that what you'd prefer to be called? Abby?"

I swallowed and nodded. Mama poked me with her mind-your-manners elbow.

"Yes, ma'am," I said. "I only get called Abigail when I'm in big trouble."

Mama's face turned red. The lady laughed. It was a nice laugh.

She held out her hand. "I'm Miss Bettis. I'll be your homeroom teacher and your English teacher."

I took her hand. It was cool and soft. "I'm Abby Whistler."

After she and Mama made their hellos, Miss Bettis said, "Let's get you down to homeroom so you can meet everybody. Does that sound like a good idea?"

"Yes ma'am," I said. I figured if everybody at Jesse Rogers Middle School was as nice as she was, I might get along okay.

Miss Bettis steered me out into the mass of kids.

"I'll pick you up after school, Abby," Mama hollered over all the noise.

It seemed like it took forever and a day to get to the classroom. I figured you could have put three of my school at Harmony Gap into this one school, it was so big.

Finally, Miss Bettis stopped in front of room 309. "Here we go," she said.

She pulled open the door and gave me a little nudge.

My mouth must've fell open all the way to the ground. I stared at the huge room with all its computers and bulletin boards and fish tanks and bookshelves and about a million and one eyes staring at me.

"Better close your mouth before a fly gets in," someone called. Laughter rippled across the room.

Miss Bettis frowned. Everyone went quiet. "Class, we have a new student joining us. This is Abby Whistler." Not a single person said hey.

"Abby, why don't you tell us all where you're from?"

I glanced at the kids in the front of the class. They looked like they could care less where I came from.

"Um . . . Harmony Gap, North Carolina," I said, staring down at my feet like they were the most fascinating things on the planet.

"Well, that sounds like a lovely place," Miss Bettis said. "But I'm sure you'll be happy here in Nashville, right, class?"

Not a peep out of anybody, just lots of eye rolling and shrugging. At that particular moment, I wanted a big ol' hole to open up in the floor and swallow me up.

Miss Bettis guided me over to a desk by the only window in the class. "I think we'll put you here, Abby."

I slid into my desk and tried to make myself very, very small.

She motioned to the girl sitting next to me who was busy smearing shiny stuff on her lips.

"Madison, would you serve as Abby's escort this week?"

The girl glanced over at me. "Sure thing, Miss B." She popped her gum. I waited for Miss Bettis to tell her to address her by her proper name and to get rid of that gum.

But she didn't. Instead, she smiled and said, "Thank you, Madison. Make sure she finds her classes and the cafeteria."

Without sparing me a glance, Madison said, "Sure, whatever." If that had been Mrs. Radley at my old school, she would have jerked a knot in that girl's tail for talking that way to an adult.

I took a deep breath and tried to smile just a little at Madison.

The bell rang. Madison stood up and slung a fancy-looking pack with all kinds of doodads hanging off it onto her shoulder. "Let's go," she said.

"See you back here for English, Abby," Miss Bettis called.

Madison held out her hand. "Let's see your schedule."

I handed the crumpled piece of paper over to her.

She frowned as she smoothed it out. "You need to take good care of this," she said.

"Why?" I asked.

"Because it's got everything on it—your class schedule, your locker number and combination—"

"I got a locker?" I asked. I'd never had a locker before.

Only the kids at the Balsam County High School got lockers.

"Of course you have a locker," she said.

"What do I do with a locker?" I asked.

She studied me like I was a bug under a windowpane. "I can see I have my work cut out for me."

"Abby! Abby, over here!" Mama waved and hollered at me from the parking lot. The end of my first day at Jesse Rogers Middle School and my head was about to bust.

I slid into the seat beside Mama, slammed the car door closed. For the first time that day, everything was quiet.

Mama touched my cheek. "You okay?"

"Yes, Mama. I believe I am."

She smiled and pulled out of the parking lot. "So how was your first day of school?"

Every single crack and crease of my brain was full to overflowing with everything about the day, so finding the right words was hard. "Okay, I reckon," was all my brain had room for.

"Was it a lot different from your old school?"

I laughed. "It purely was," I said. "The kids dress different, talk different, and act different. And Mama, we change classes lots more than we did at Harmony Gap."

"Is that so?" she said.

"Uh-huh. And my history teacher is black and my

123

math teacher is from somewhere in India. I can't pro-
nounce his name, but he's real nice. I'm ahead of the other
kids in the class."

"You got your daddy's math gene," she said. "So your
day must've gone by fast, then?"

"Yes, it did. I can't even recall . . ."

And then it hit me like a ton of bricks: I'd gone a whole
eight hours without thinking about Tam. Not once.

"What's wrong, honey?"

I blinked back tears. "Nothing," I said. "I reckon I'm
just tired."

We pulled up into the driveway of our rented house.
My heart sagged just like the front screen door. Patches of
paint curled away from the wood. The porch was barely
big enough for one chair. When we first saw this house,
Daddy said the yard was small enough for a feller to pee
across. That had made me and Mama laugh.

Mama sat there beside me looking at the house too.
Neither of us said anything for a long moment. Finally
she sighed and squeezed my hand. "Let's go in and unpack
some more boxes."

Later that night, after pizza and Daddy's stories about all
the people he was meeting down at the recording studio,
I went to my tiny little room to unpack another box. I
unpacked the last of my books and sketches. I put Tam's

picture on the table by my bed. I hung his collar from the bedpost.

Somewhere close by, another siren wailed. I'd never in my entire life heard so many sirens and cars and horns honking and people yelling. I missed hearing the wind in the old oak tree and the hoot owls late at night. I missed hearing Meemaw's clear, strong voice drifting up through the heat vents from the kitchen below.

I crawled into my bed and pulled one of Meemaw's quilts around my legs. From my bedside table, I took out Olivia's letter. I unfolded it and read it for the fifty-second time.

Dear Abby,

You are the best friend I've ever had and I'll miss you very much. But I want you to be with your parents. They need you. My papa used to always say the earth only spins one way: forward.

Try to be happy, okay?

Your friend always,

Olivia

"Just like Olivia," I said to no one in particular. "Short and sweet."

I threw off the quilt and ran to find Mama, which wasn't hard in such a tiny house.

"Mama, have you got your computer set up yet?"

She looked up from the box of dishes. "Yes, it's in the living room. Why?"

"Mama," I said, "can you teach me how to do email?"

CHAPTER 22

Tam

Ivy Calhoun had lived outside of Galax, Virginia, near the banks of the New River, ever since most people could remember. Her daddy had built the cabin back in the twenties, when he'd bought the old Sawyer Mill and the forty acres around it. Folks had come from miles around to grind their corn and wheat, taking home sacks full of flour, cornmeal, and grits. Local legend had it that a fair amount of moonshine was bought from the Sawyer Mill too. That wouldn't have surprised Ivy at all. Her daddy was fond of saying, "A man's got to do what he has to do to feed his family." And he had fed them well. There had been Ivy and her big brothers, Samuel and Ben; her older sister, Iris; and the middle child, Rose. Ivy was the baby.

Ivy shook her head as she pushed herself out of the worn leather chair by the fire. "I'll be eighty-two come spring, and I still think of myself as 'the baby,'" she said to no one in particular. She glanced at the faded black-and-white photographs on the fireplace mantel. The mill had been silent for forty years or more now. The great, groaning wheel was still. The cabin, like herself, showed its age. But the river and the mountains and the land were the same as ever.

Ivy pulled on her boots and grabbed the walking stick her grandson had carved for her at camp. She stuffed a bag of stale bread crumbs in her coat pocket.

It was her custom when the weather was good to walk the perimeter of the property, just like her daddy had done every day she could remember. It drove her children crazy.

"What if you were to fall and break a hip or something?" her daughter would say almost every Sunday during their weekly phone visit.

"You don't know what all kind of weirdos might be out there by the river, Mama," her son would say. He was a police officer in Roanoke. He thought everybody was a weirdo. Between those two and her nosy neighbors, Ivy Calhoun didn't get a moment's peace.

She stepped out onto the porch and squinted up into the winter sky. "Still," she said, "I suppose they mean well."

The sun touched the top of the ridge across the hollow.

New snow sugared the trees. She watched the ridgeline grow brighter and brighter. When Ivy was a child, she'd stood on this same porch every morning with her daddy and watched this same sight. "It's coming alive, baby girl," he'd say. And it was true.

Beyond that ridge, thirty or forty miles to the east, wound the Blue Ridge Parkway. She and her husband used to drive up to the craggy balds where the best blueberries grew. Ivy smiled. "That man was a fool for blueberry pie," she said to the brightening sky.

First she walked the fence line along the high pasture. The snow from two days before had melted in the open sun. A cardinal, bright red and black-masked head, watched Ivy from a fence post. Her husband used to say there was no prettier sight on God's green earth than a cardinal in the snow. That was true too.

Ivy picked her way down into the forest, careful of her footing. She followed the winding line of dogwood and redbud trees. Ivy reached into her coat pocket and pulled out the plastic bag of stale bread crumbs. "Come get breakfast," she called to the birds as she scattered the crumbs upon the snow.

The ground leveled as she approached the bank of the river. The water was narrow and shallow here. Her children had spent many a summer day on these banks looking for salamanders and crawdaddies. Farther down, where the river widened, the children had caught trout. Ivy knew where wild onions were plentiful in the spring and where the wild asparagus grew.

The old woman walked along the river, careful of slippery rocks buried beneath snow and dead leaves. Lids of ice capped the water pooled in the small, still places.

As she started up the gentle slope leading away from the river, something caught Ivy's eye. It looked like a pile of old leaves or perhaps some garbage washed up from the river. She was about to walk on when a raven landed on the ground right in front of her. It cawed in agitation.

"What do you want, you noisy old thing?" Ivy knew this particular raven by his oddly notched tail feathers.

The bird hopped over to the pile on the riverbank, raised his wings up and down, and cawed louder. Ivy watched the raven's strange behavior. Finally she said, "Oh all right, all right," and made her way back down the bank.

"Oh my," she breathed, bending down to get a better look. "What happened to you, you poor little fox?" Her daddy had hated foxes because they ate the chickens. But Ivy hadn't had chickens on the place for years. She took great pleasure in watching the foxes slip quietly through her front yard and hunt the fields.

An ear twitched at the sound of her voice. An eye opened and locked on her face. Without thinking, Ivy lowered herself to the ground. "Why, you're no fox," she gasped. "You're a dog!" She ran her hand carefully along the wet, matted coat. Bones rippled beneath her hand. Blood stained her glove. The dog whimpered. Tears stung Ivy's eyes. "You poor, poor thing," she whispered.

Snow drifted down around her as she stood. She looked up. The sky had turned from blue to lead gray. A gust of wind blew open her coat. "I've got to get you up to the cabin," she said. She studied the size of the dog and the distance to the cabin. She heard her daughter's voice, "*Honestly*, Mama! What are you *thinking*?" She heard the raven call from the tree above.

Ivy set her jaw, dropped her walking stick, and scooped up the dog. "Why, you're nothing but skin and bones," she said as she carried Tam up the slope to the cabin.

In no time, Tam lay on a wool blanket in the leather chair before the fire. The snow came down hard now, burying the front yard and piling against the house. A fretful wind howled across the chimney, but inside the cabin it was warm and dry.

Ivy watched the snow, one hand stroking Tam's head. "If ever there was a dog in need of a vet it's you. But I don't dare drive in this storm. I'd get us both killed for sure, and then I'd never hear the end of it from my daughter."

Ivy pulled up the footstool and sat down next to Tam.

She put on her glasses for a better look. After her husband had died, she'd worked as a nurse's assistant at the hospital in Galax. The old woman had helped put back together more folks than she cared to remember.

Ivy gently parted the bloody, matted hair on Tam's shoulder. She inspected the wound, then sighed. "Looks like the shot hit your shoulder bone and came out. That's lucky. We got to get you sewn up, though, so you don't lose any more blood than you already have."

Ivy checked Tam from nose to tail, then, as carefully as she could, rolled him over. "Oh dear," she said with a sigh. Ivy peered at the angry, infected abscess. She'd seen this often enough back when she'd had dogs of her own. "Just like I thought. You've had a run-in with a porcupine.

"Well," she said, heading to the kitchen, "I got my work cut out for me."

It was still snowing that night as Ivy sat, exhausted, in her rocking chair beside the fire. She had shaved the hair away from Tam's shoulder, cleaned and disinfected the gunshot wound, and sewn it up.

Removing the festering quill was harder. First, she lanced and drained the abscess, then cut into the cheek to find the quill. Once she'd dug it out, she washed and stitched his face. It was clear, though, that the dog's body was full of infection. In his near-starved state, she wondered if he had the strength to fight it.

Ivy stood and rubbed the ache in the small of her back. She pulled a fleece blanket across the dog. "I have my doubts whether or not you'll make it through the night," she said. "But if you're still alive in the morning, I'll call Doc Pritchett and see if he can come take a look at you."

The wind pushed against the walls of the cabin. Snow scratched hungrily at the windowpanes.

CHAPTER 23

Abby

To: omcbuttars@carolinanet.com
From: "Abby Whistler" <sheltiegirl@carolinanet.com>
Date: Wed, January 6 7:32 pm
Subject: Hey again from Nashville
Hey Olivia,

Thanks for sending me that email right away the other night! I can't believe how fast we can write each other. It's almost like talking on the phone. I'm glad you and your granddaddy are going to see Meemaw this weekend. I miss her something terrible! You too! Mama says our family is a lot like a three-legged dog without Meemaw. We get along okay, but we don't work nearly as well together without her.

You asked what the kids are like at my new school. The girls all dress up like they're famous country music stars—short, flouncy skirts and cowboy boots. Lots of jewelry. Even the girls in my grade wear makeup and have pierced ears! They're nice, but they mostly talk about shopping. The boys all have this hair that looks like it's blown by a good, stiff wind to one side. I think the boys spend as much time on their hair as the girls do! Ha! The weirdest thing is, during recess, all the kids just stand around texting each other on their cell phones, playing Game Boys by themselves or listening to music on their tiny little iPods. They don't play dodgeball or four-square or anything. It's boring. My teachers are nice, though, especially my homeroom teacher, Miss Bettis. She's my English teacher too. She has the nicest smile of anybody.

Oh, Olivia, I had the WORST dream about Tam a couple of nights ago! In my dream, he was lost and cold in the woods. He hardly looked like himself, but I could tell he was looking for me. I called and called to him, but he couldn't hear me. All of a sudden, this big black thing—kind of like a bear—started chasing him. Then it turned into a man and started shooting at Tam. I screamed and screamed until Mama came in and woke me up. I think I gave her a real scare. And even though it's been a couple of days, I just can't seem to shake that dream.

I better do my homework. The teachers here think

I'm real smart. That's a first! I told my math teacher the smartest person I know is named Olivia and she lives in Harmony Gap. Ha!

Write me soon. I miss you.

Your friend,

Abby Whistler

By the end of my second week at Jesse Rogers Middle School, I didn't get lost finding my classes anymore. I remembered my locker number and combination. I didn't really need Madison to escort me around, but I was actually glad she still did. She was as different from me as a pickle is from a pear. But she was smart and knew just about everybody in sixth grade.

We were eating our lunch together as usual. She and her friend Bree pored over some teen fashion magazine. Every now and then, they'd eye me, then study a picture in the magazine and say, "We could do that to her hair," or "Green would bring out those gray eyes of hers."

I wadded up my paper bag. "I am *not* y'all's latest makeover project."

Bree smiled, her lips all shiny with pink stuff. "But you could look so pretty, Abby."

Madison sighed. "And no one wears their hair like that anymore. It's so, so . . . well, hillbilly."

If there's anything I hate, it's being called a hillbilly. I was just about to tell her what she could do with her precious magazine when Bree said, "Oh my gosh, there she is!"

Madison gasped. "So it's true. She *is* coming to this school."

Bree and Madison and just about everybody else in the cafeteria, including the lunch ladies, stared at the girl who'd just walked in. She didn't look that much different from all the other girls at the school, except maybe a little taller and dressed all in black, from head to toe. She had on these clunky army-type boots with all kinds of buckles and laces and such.

"Who's she?" I asked.

Bree and Madison said at the same time, "Cheyenne Rivers."

I looked back at the girl strutting over to the salad bar. Kids moved out of her way, like Moses parting the Red Sea.

"Why is she such a big deal?" I asked.

They looked at me like I'd suddenly sprouted two heads. "You don't know who Cheyenne Rivers is?"

I shook my head. Madison rolled her eyes. "She's *Randy Rivers's* daughter."

"Please tell me you know who Randy Rivers is," Bree said. Sometimes Bree had a way of talking like I was from another planet.

"Of course I know who Randy Rivers is," I said, even

though I didn't. But in this city, if anybody was some-body, they had to be a country-western singer, so I figured that's who Randy Rivers was.

So I said, just like I knew what I was talking about, "What's the daughter of a rich and famous country music star doing at a public school?"

Without peeling one eyeball off the girl, Madison said, "I heard she's been kicked out of every private school in Nashville."

Bree nodded. "I heard they hired a tutor for her at home, but she was so hateful, she ran the teacher off."

I watched this Cheyenne Rivers walk over to an empty table by the windows, never looking right or left. She carried herself like the Queen of England.

"She doesn't look so bad," I said.

They looked at me and shook their heads. "I heard practically everyone in eighth grade is making bets on how long it'll take for her to get kicked out."

Bree and Madison pretended to read their magazine while they watched Cheyenne Rivers. "I heard her mother takes her to New York City six times a year just to shop for clothes," Bree said.

"I heard she has a boyfriend who's *eighteen*," Madison said.

One thing I know from living in a small town where everybody thinks they know everybody else's business is most of what is said about a person is just pure exaggeration. I watched this famous girl sitting over there by the window all by herself. It didn't look to me like her teacher in the eighth grade had thought to give her an escort, like Miss Bettis did for me. Nobody said hey or welcome to our school. I felt sorry for her.

I slid into the truck next to Mama that afternoon when school was out. "Mama," I said, "do you know who Randy Rivers is?"

Mama peered through the rain and sleet lashing the windshield. "I hate this weather," she grumbled.

Mama didn't seem like she was in the best mood in the world, so I figured I'd better keep my mouth shut and let her drive. Mama had not been the happiest person since we'd moved to Nashville. Oh, when Daddy was home, she tried real hard to act happy. But when it was just us—and with Daddy at the studio so much, that was most of the time—she sighed a lot and looked sad. And not being able to find a job wasn't helping her general disposition either.

We pulled into the parking lot of the Harris Teeter grocery store. Mama just sat there, watching the windshield wipers going back and forth, back and forth. I touched her arm. "Mama, are we going in?"

She looked at me and blinked, then turned off the

wipers and smiled. But it wasn't her real, I'm-happy-to-be-alive smile.

She touched my cheek. "Sorry, Abby. Let's go in and see if they have some of that good fried chicken for dinner. Your dad won't be home until later and I don't feel like cooking just for us."

Me and Mama had already had Harris Teeter fried chicken for supper twice that week, and I surely was not eager to have it again. But I didn't have the heart to tell Mama that.

I hugged the warm, greasy bag of chicken pieces to my stomach while we wandered the grocery aisles. I tugged on Mama's sleeve and said, "Mama, do you know who Randy Rivers is?"

Mama tossed some boxes of cereal in our basket. "Sure, he's a real famous country-western singer. Why?"

"His daughter just started at our school," I said.

"Really?" she said. "I'd think a rich kid like that would go to some fancy-schmancy private school."

I grabbed a box of Nilla Wafers and slipped them in the basket. "She did, but you know what?"

Mama shook her head, her long braid switching back and forth. Madison and Bree would want to give her a makeover too.

"They say she's gotten kicked out of every private school there is, Mama, and she had a tutor at home and she was so mean, she ran him off. Our school," I whispered, "is a *last resort*."

Mama frowned. "You know as well as I do that you can't believe half of what people say, especially about other folks. She's probably lonely, just like everybody else."

"I know," I said. "I was thinking that too. Nobody at school will talk to her or even go near her. It's kind of sad," I said.

Mama stopped and looked down at me and smiled. "I bet you will."

"Me?" I said. But, truly, sometimes it was downright scary how well Mama knew me.

The next day in the cafeteria, I watched for Cheyenne Rivers. As usual, Madison and Bree and another friend of theirs were busy dissecting the way everybody in school dressed and how they acted.

Just when I'd about given up on her, Cheyenne Rivers appeared in the door of the cafeteria. And again, the whole noisy place went stone quiet.

She sashayed over to the salad bar and tossed a few things on her tray. Then she made her way over to that table by the window, not once looking at anybody, just like before.

She sat down, opened a book, and took a bite of apple. Madison sighed. "She's so cool."

"Totally," Bree said.

"Beyond cool," their friend Courtney said.

"Then why don't you go say hey to her?" I asked.

They looked at me like I'd asked why they didn't go peek into the boy's bathroom.

I threw up my hands. "Great bucket of gravy."

I could feel a million eyes watching me as I walked over to Cheyenne Rivers's table. The closer I got, the more it seemed like this was not such a bright idea. Then I remembered Mama saying, *She's probably lonely, just like everybody else.*

I took a deep breath and walked right up to her. "Hey," I said.

Without even looking up from her book, she said, "Hey." But it wasn't a hey-I'm-happy-to-meet-you kind of hey. It was more like a go-away-and-leave-me-alone hey.

"My name's Abby Whistler," I said.

She looked up from her book and glared around the cafeteria with narrow, mean eyes. "So who put you up to this?"

I shuffled my feet. "Nobody," I said. "It's just, I'm new here too, and I thought—"

She looked back down at her book and waved me away like an annoying fly. "Stop thinking and scram."

My mouth fell open, and my face turned hot. Who the heck did she think she was? I balled up my fists and said,

"Just because you got a rich and famous daddy doesn't give you the right to be rude. My Mama would jerk a knot in your tail for talking that way to someone offering kindness."

She closed her book, sat back in her chair, and took me in. There I was, a scrawny little sixth grader with long braids, baggy jeans, and a flannel shirt, who didn't matter a toot, telling the Queen she was rude. Right then and there, I wanted a big ol' hole to open up and swallow me up.

She smiled like a cat fixing to eat a mouse. She opened her mouth to say something . . .

And the bell rang.

I never made it so fast from lunch to history before.

CHAPTER 24

Tam

Tam's feet twitched fitfully in his sleep. He dreamed the foul-smelling man with the long black rifle chased him through a meadow. No matter how fast he ran, the man was always there, just behind. Tam called and called for the coyote, but she never answered. In his dream, Tam tore across a wide-open meadow. The man raised his rifle. *Crack!* Something slammed into his body, knocking him to the ground.

Tam jerked awake, heart pounding against his ribs. He heard a loud pop and then a crack. Struggling, he lifted his head. An old woman fed wood into the fireplace by the chair where he lay, safe. He lowered his head, exhausted.

Ivy turned and wiped her hands on her pants. She

smiled when she saw Tam's brown eyes fixed on her face. "You made it through the night, little boy. You're one tough cookie." She reached down to stroke his head. Tam jerked away from her touch, fear filling his eyes.

Ivy pulled her hand away. "It's okay, boy. I know I won't hurt you, but *you* don't know that. You just rest a little bit longer before I see to your wounds." Her gentle voice brought a familiar feeling to Tam. He didn't quite know what it was, but he knew enough that he could go back to sleep.

The next time Tam awoke, it was to the sound of wind and the delicious smell of food.

He couldn't see Ivy, but he could hear her rummaging around the kitchen.

"Aha! Found it!" She bustled over to Tam's bed in the old leather chair. She held a bowl filled with a wonderful smell. "I cooked up some of my mama's special Get Well Soup. She always made this when one of us kids was sick in bed. Always seemed to do the trick, so I don't see why it shouldn't work on you."

She held the bowl up to Tam's nose for a sniff. He tried to lift his head to drink, but the side of his face was still too swollen and painful. He lay his head back down on the towel with a whimper.

"I thought so," Ivy said. "So I devised a plan B." She placed the open end of a turkey baster in the bowl, released the rubber bulb at the other end, and sucked up a tube full of soup. Gently, she slipped her hand under the sheltie's head and tipped up his muzzle. She pried his mouth open just a bit and slipped the turkey baster in. Slowly, she released the warm soup. At first, it dribbled out the side just like the night before. But Tam had gotten the taste of the soup. The second time she placed the baster in his mouth, he swallowed hungrily, warmth filling his mouth and spreading through his body.

"Good boy," Ivy said. "Let's see if we can get a little more down you." Tam finished half the bowl.

Ivy placed the bowl on the table next to the chair and stroked the white star on the top of Tam's head. "You're not going to like what comes next, little friend. But I got to see to those wounds of yours." She gazed out the window. "Storm's still going strong out there. No way Doc Pritchett can get out here. So," she said, giving him a final pat on the head, "looks like it's up to me."

She turned on the lamp beside the chair and moved it so it shone down on Tam's side. She pulled back the fleece blanket and parted the hair on his shoulder. Tam jerked his head up in alarm as she touched the painful place.

"Lie still, honey," Ivy said in a soothing voice. It was a voice she had used many times to calm hurt and frightened patients and children. "I won't hurt you," she said. Tam lay his head back down and gave himself up to her.

The cut she'd made the night before to clean the bullet wound looked good. At least there was no sign of infection. The skin around the stitches looked red but not unduly so. She smeared antibiotic ointment around the area, then pulled the blanket back up. She sighed. "Don't know if I should put a bandage over that shoulder or not. Seems like as long as you're not moving around, the air is the best thing for it."

Next she checked his face. The swelling had gone down a bit, but the abscess where the quill had embedded in his cheek was still draining. His cheek felt hot to the touch. Ivy cleaned the drainage from his face with a warm rag. "I just don't know about this," she said. "I sure wish it looked better."

She and Tam studied each other for a moment, then she stood. "Well, I can at least try and call the doctor."

Doc Pritchett picked up on the second ring. After he and Ivy had asked after each other's health and remarked on the storm, Ivy told him about Tam.

"Well, it sounds like you got your hands full, Mrs. Calhoun," the old vet said with just a trace of laughter in his voice.

"Don't you dare tell me I'm too old to be taking in a hurt stray," Ivy scolded. "You're older than me and you still got those sheep of yours."

Doc Pritchett laughed. "I've known you too long, Ivy

Calhoun. I wouldn't dare tell you what to do and *not* do!" When Ivy didn't answer, he cleared his throat. "If I could, I'd come straightaway and see to this little dog," he said. "But seeing as how I can't, what with the roads being closed and all, and the weatherman calling for still more snow . . ."

Ivy sighed. "Just tell me what to do, you chattering old fool."

After he'd finished laughing, he said, "Sounds like you've handled things pretty well so far. I trust you to know whether or not there was a bullet still in his shoulder, and you stitched up many a patient."

"It's where I had to dig out the quill I'm worried about," Ivy said. "It's still infected."

"Probably is," the vet agreed. "Keep wet heat on it to draw out as much of the infection as you can. It's actually a good thing that the abscess is able to drain on its own. If it closes back up, though, you'll have to lance it." After a quiet second, he asked, "You been able to get any food into him?" She explained about her mama's special soup and the turkey baster.

Doc Pritchett laughed and laughed. "Ivy Calhoun, if you don't beat all!"

Before they hung up, he said, "I'll check back in with you later tonight, see how your patient is doing. If this storm ever stops and the roads get cleared, I'll come on out and take a look at him."

Ivy stood at the kitchen window and watched the curtains of white snow blow across the meadow. "I'm just glad I found him when I did," she said.

"Yep," the vet said. "He's one lucky dog."

Two days later, Doc Pritchett stood over Tam, who was laid out on blankets and towels on the dining room table. Ivy held a flashlight above with one hand and stroked Tam's ears with the other.

"You're right," he said, gently pressing Tam's shoulder. "There's no bullet in here, although doubtless there was one. The wound looks fine. No sign of infection. Stitches look good."

"Do you think there's any bone or tissue damage?" Ivy asked.

"Hard to say," the vet said, straightening up. "Won't really know until he gets up and starts moving around. Bone could have been chipped. I think if there were any torn muscles or ligaments there'd be more swelling.

"This face, on the other hand, is where the infection is," he said, bending back over Tam. "I'm going to give him a shot of painkiller and sedative, open this back up, and clean out the infected tissue." He sighed. "It would be better to do this in a disinfected office under general anesthesia." He peered into Ivy's eyes.

She shook her head. "Lord only knows what all's happened to this poor creature. I don't want to cause him any more fear. Let's just do it." The vet sighed again and opened his leather medical bag.

An hour later, Tam was back in the leather chair before the fire, sleeping. Ivy and Doc Pritchett sat at the dining room table sipping tea.

"What do you think his chances are?" Ivy asked.

Blowing across the top of his cup to cool the hot tea, the vet said, "Pretty good, I think. That shot of antibiotic should go a long ways toward knocking out the infection. I'll give him another at the end of the week." Glancing in the direction of the chair, he said, "The main thing is to get some food into him. He hasn't got a thing to him."

Later, as the old man pulled on his coat and scarf, he looked down at Tam. "Hard to tell looking at him now, but he could be a Shetland sheepdog. Or at least part. If he is, he'll make you a good companion. They're smart as a whip and loyal as they come."

"But why in the world would a dog like that be washed up half dead on the banks of the New River with a gunshot wound?"

Doc Pritchett reached down and stroked Tam's side. "Who knows. From the looks of him, I'd say he hasn't been someone's dog in a long while. He's seen some hard times."

"Maybe I should take him in to town to see if anyone recognizes him or to see if he's got one of those microchips. Someone could be looking for him right now," Ivy said, not really believing it herself.

As if reading her mind, the vet shook his head. "Whoever would let a dog get in this kind of shape doesn't deserve him. Besides," he said, bending down and looking at Tam's feet, "this dog has been traveling for many miles in rough terrain."

"Why do you say that?" Ivy asked.

"Just look at his pads," the old vet said, running his thumb over the crosshatched scars and tears on Tam's pads. "They tell the whole story."

CHAPTER 25

Abby

To: omcbuttars@carolinanet.com
From: "Abby Whistler" <sheltiegirl@carolinanet.com>
Date: Sat, January 23 10:32 am
Subject: Hey again from Nashville

Hey Olivia,

In English class Friday, Miss Bettis said we have to read a book that won the Newbery Award. I told her I don't know what that is, and she took me to the school library and showed me where they're all shelved. She said a couple of them were about dogs, and maybe I'd like to read one of those. So I brought home a book called _Old Yeller_. Have you read it? Do you think I'll like it?

I'm bored. Mama FINALLY got a part-time job, but she has to work every other Saturday. This coffee shop where she's working makes her work some nights and Saturdays. She never had to do that at Mr. Billy's Feed and Seed back home. I don't think Mama likes working at this place.

I did get invited to a party today. These girls I know at school—Madison, Bree, and Courtney—are having a makeover party. I'm not entirely sure what a makeover party is, but I think it involves a lot of goop on your face, swapping clothes, and doing all kinds of things to each other's hair. When I got invited to that party, I got two big surprises: One was that I even got invited to a party and the other was I actually kind of wanted to go. But Mama needed the truck for work, and Daddy's van (as usual) isn't running right, so I couldn't go. I don't know what's wrong with me that I'm sad I couldn't go.

Oh, Daddy just said he needs to go to the recording studio for a while and he wants me to go with him!

Your friend,

Abby Whistler

I skipped along beside Daddy as we walked to the recording studio. Daddy had his favorite guitar slung over his back, and I carried his mandolin.

The studio wasn't far from our house. It was in a real famous area called Music Row. It kind of looked like a neighborhood, except most all the houses were actually recording studios. Only the really big studios, like Sony, were in fancy, official-looking buildings.

I liked Daddy's recording studio. It was a happy-looking, purple wooden house with a nice porch on the front. It looked like a house made for music.

But inside, it didn't look like anybody's house. There was a receptionist's desk when you first came in and a tiny little kitchen back behind the desk. The rest of the house was made up of soundproof rooms, the room where a guy sits behind this big instrument panel with all kinds of lights and switches, and offices. Everywhere, there were photographs of famous musicians who've recorded there.

The other guys in Daddy's band—Tommy and Jeb Stuart, and Cue Ball—tuned their guitars and bass fiddle in one of those soundproof rooms.

"Hey, Half Pint," Tommy Stuart said when we walked in. Tommy was always teasing me.

"Hey, Big Foot," I said back. I called him Big Foot because of the fact he's so hairy on his head and arms and legs.

"You going to help us out today?" Cue Ball asked. The lights in the studio shined something fierce off his bald head.

"That's not a bad idea," Daddy said, taking his mandolin from its case. "But for now, she's going to sit over there in the corner and be real quiet, right, sugar?"

"Sure thing, Daddy."

I hopped up on a stool over in the corner. I had a million

and three questions about how all the things worked, but I zipped up my mouth instead.

"Okay, gentlemen, you ready?" a voice asked from the other side of a smoky glass wall.

Daddy looked at Jeb, Tommy, and Cue Ball. They all nodded. "We're all set, Mike," Daddy said.

Daddy tapped his toes three times and counted down real soft, "One, two, three, and . . ."

And just like always, the Clear Creek Boys carried me away. I forgot I was in this tiny little room in Nashville, Tennessee. As Daddy sang his own special version of "The Water Is Wide," I felt like I was right back on our porch way up in Wild Cat Cove. My fingers itched, though, for my own guitar, and I wanted to raise my voice and sing along with them.

Then they did some old Irish songs that liked to spin me out of my seat. Daddy looked like a wild man with that fiddle. After that, they slowed it down with one of Jeb's songs and then one of Daddy's. I was in pure-tee heaven.

"That's great," the guy called from behind the glass wall. "Take a break."

I jumped off the stool and ran over to Daddy. "Daddy, can I see what that guy is doing in that room?"

Daddy looked toward the glass. "Hey, Mike, is it okay if I bring my girl in?"

"Sure thing."

I felt like Dorothy in *The Wizard of Oz*, seeing what all the Wizard really did behind that curtain.

Mike showed me how he could mix the music he recorded. He could bring out the voices if he wanted to and soften the fiddle. He could make the music sound sharp and clear as cut glass or rich and smoky like the mountains at dusk.

"How many more we need to do?" Daddy asked.

"Mr. Katz wants six cuts for the demo disk, so you need to do two more," Mike said.

We headed back into the recording room. Daddy and the rest of the guys talked about what songs to do. "Let's have some fun with these last two," Tommy said. Tommy always wanted things to be fun, which was something I liked a lot about him.

"How about 'Big Rock Candy Mountain'?" Cue Ball said. "That one's fun."

I wiggled on my stool. "I love that one, Daddy."

Daddy looked over at me and grinned. "I know you do, peanut, so why don't you grab my guitar and join us?"

I tell you, my jaw dropped straight down into my lap. "Really, Daddy?"

"Really and truly," he said with a grin as wide as the world.

I held Daddy's guitar like it was a newborn baby. I had never played it before. It was so much bigger than my little Gibson guitar.

Daddy tuned up his banjo, Jeb settled his fiddle on his shoulder, and Tommy would play the other guitar while Cue Ball played his bass fiddle.

"Ready for us, Mike?" Daddy called.

And off we went, picking and singing and having a good time. With each stanza, we went faster and faster. By the time we came to the end, we all had a fit of giggles.

Then we decided to slow it down with a Meemaw favorite, "Down to the River to Pray."

> *As I went down to the river to pray*
> *Studyin' about that good ol' way*

I imagined Meemaw there with us, playing her harpsichord or her dulcimer, her voice strong and clear as Clear Creek itself. I expected any minute to hear—

"Who the heck is that?"

My eyes flew open. Someone stood on the other side of the glass with Mike, squinting out at us.

"Uh-oh," Jeb said. Everybody stopped playing and singing.

"Whistler," a not-too-friendly voice boomed from behind the glass.

I saw Daddy swallow hard. "Yes, sir, Mr. Katz?"

"Do you have a new band member I don't know about?"

Daddy ran his hand through his hair. "This is my

daughter, Abby." Motioning to the glass, Daddy said to me, "Abby, honey, say hey to our boss, Mr. Katz."

I lifted a hand. "Hey, Mr. Katz. How are you?"

Silence.

I personally thought it was rude, him not coming out to introduce himself. Meemaw would accuse him of being raised in a barn. There was a long silence. Finally Mr. Katz said, "Whistler, meet me in my office."

I mean to tell you, Daddy looked like a puppy that'd been caught peeing on the carpet. He slipped off his banjo, smoothed down his shirt, and gave us all a weak smile. "Wish me luck."

To: omcbuttars@carolinanet.com
From: "Abby Whistler" <sheltiegirl@carolinanet.com>
Date: Saturday, Jan 23, 8:24 pm
Subject: Daddy

Hey,

Boy, did Daddy get in trouble today! He took me with him to the recording studio where he and the band are cutting a demo disk. Everything was going along just fine—I sat real quiet in the studio while they recorded their songs. I even got to see how the songs get mixed on the disk and stuff. It was really cool! Then Daddy had me play the guitar and sing on the last two songs. I tell you, Olivia, it was the most fun and the best I'd felt since we got to this city. I closed my eyes and pretended I was back on our porch in Wild Cat Cove. And then, all of a sudden, Daddy's boss, the one who owns the studio, shows up and gets his underwear all in a knot because I was playing and singing on their demo. He called Daddy down to his office and everything! I felt so bad for him when he came back. He looked like how I felt when I failed that big history test last year. He was real quiet on the walk home. He didn't sing or make jokes or anything. Later, I overheard him tell Mama that not only was Mr. Katz mad about me being on the disk, but he also didn't like that we were playing old-timey, traditional stuff. "He wants us to play more modern, pop-type songs. Not traditional mountain songs." Poor Daddy. He sounded so miserable when he said "mountain songs." That's what Daddy loves. Just like your grandpa.

Oh, thanks for warning me about that book *Old Yeller*. I do NOT want to read a book where the dog gets killed off in the end! Yes, let's do read the same book. I'll ask Miss Bettis to help me find a different book when I get to school on Monday.

I sure do miss you, Olivia.

Abby

P.S. I haven't had any dreams about Tam for a long time. What do you think that means?

CHAPTER 26

Tam

Three weeks after finding Tam on the banks of the New River, Ivy couldn't imagine life without him. She talked to him constantly, read sections of the newspaper aloud to him. She knew she could be mistaken, but it did seem to her he took a keen interest in the sports section. They sat together before the fire, her with her knitting, him with some new toy she tried to interest him in.

Ivy was just finishing reading the last of the sports page to Tam when the phone rang.

It was her daughter, Caroline.

"Yes, honey, I know I haven't called in a while. I've been busy." She nodded, then looked at Tam and rolled her eyes.

"I know you worry, honey, and I appreciate that, but I'm fine. Really."

"Come up there this weekend? Well, I don't think I can. Not right now." Tam could hear what sounded like the chattering of an angry squirrel. He whined, his eyes searching Ivy's face.

Ivy stroked Tam's ears, then said, "It's just I have a sick friend I'm taking care of. He can't do much for himself right now. He's been down for a while and—"

"Now, Caroline, I may be old, but I'm still perfectly capable of helping a friend in need." Straightening her shoulders, Ivy said in a firm voice, "I will call you in a few days, honey. And then I'll get up there when I can."

"Honestly," Ivy said, hanging up the phone and snapping open the paper. "Now where were we?"

A week passed. On an unusually warm day, Tam lay on the front porch, eyes closed, sun soothing his aching shoulder. One ear twitched at rustling in the dry grass of the pasture. In his dream, the coyote arced over the tall grass, ready to pounce. Tam barked his excitement for the hunt.

Ivy heard the muffled *woof*s coming from the sleeping sheltie. She watched his feet twitch, his tail thump. She smiled. "No telling what adventures you're reliving in your dreams," she said. Gently, she shook him awake.

Tam opened his eyes. For a moment he was confused

by the hard wood beneath his body, the gentle hand on his side, the kind eyes. Where was the coyote and the deep woods and the taste of hot blood?

"Come on, boy," Ivy said, standing up. "It's time we went to town." Catching the word *come*, he stood and followed the old woman to the car. A raven called to them from the branches of a dogwood tree as they pulled out of the drive, the sun glinting on its notched tail.

Tam watched the fields and trees race by the car with great interest. It had been a long time since he'd ridden inside a car, but he remembered that it almost always led somewhere exciting.

Ivy turned on the car radio, searching for a station. Tam tilted his head to one side when the sound of a fiddle and banjo leaped from the radio. Ivy smiled and stroked Tam's back. "If I didn't know better, I'd say you have a definite preference for bluegrass music."

Their first stop was the Galax post office. She patted Tam's head. "I got to run in and mail off my order for more yarn, boy. You guard the car." Tam's eyes never left the front door of the post office. He relaxed when she slid back in the front seat beside him. "Now to the bank," she said.

At the drive-up window, something stirred in Tam's memory as he watched the teller behind the glass. He licked his lips and pressed his nose to the window.

"When did you get you a dog, Mrs. Calhoun?" the girl asked as she counted out the dollar bills.

"He and I sort of found each other out in the woods a while back," Ivy said.

The girl shook her head. "I'd be careful if I was you, Mrs. Calhoun, taking in stray dogs. My daddy says there's coyotes up in the mountains, closer than you might think."

Ivy sniffed. "He's a Shetland sheepdog, Tiffany. Not a coyote."

The metal tray slid toward the car window and opened. Ivy took the cash and a dog biscuit from the tray. She handed Tam the biscuit. "Thanks, Tiffany," Ivy called as they pulled away.

Ivy watched Tam lick the last of the biscuit crumbs from the car seat. "Next stop is for you, boy," she said. "It's time to let you do some shopping." Pulling into the parking lot in front of a store called Everything Dog, Ivy muttered, "*Honestly*, coyotes.

"Well, first thing I guess," Ivy said, "is to get him a collar. What color do you think would look best on this handsome boy?" she said, looking down at Tam, nestled in her arms.

Prissy Spinks peered at him doubtfully over her glasses. "He's an odd-looking little fellow, isn't he? Kind of puny. . . ."

Hugging Tam closer to her, Ivy said, "He's a Shetland

sheepdog, Prissy. They are very smart and loyal." Tam wagged his tail and sneezed in agreement.

Brightening, Prissy Spinks pulled a green-and-black-plaid collar from the rack. "Since Shetland sheepdogs are from Scotland, I think a plaid collar would suit him, don't you?"

Next came a bright red leash, food and water bowls, more toys, rawhide chewies, and a fake sheepskin bed. Surveying the pile on the checkout counter, Ivy said, "What else? I feel like I'm forgetting something important. . . ."

"What about an identification tag for his collar, Mrs. Calhoun?"

"Of *course*," Ivy said, shaking her head. "How could I forget that?"

"I'll just put the form you need to fill out right here in the bag with your receipt. You fill that on out and bring it in. I'll mail it for you myself."

"How long does it take to get the tag?" Ivy asked as Prissy Spinks loaded the packages in the trunk of her car.

"Only a couple of weeks, is all."

That night, as Ivy filled out the form, a cold wind raced across the roof of the cabin, blowing down the chimney. "Okay, we'll have them put the address and the phone number. But we need to put your name on the tag too. What's your name? I need to call you something other than 'boy.'"

Ivy watched Tam limp over to the front door then look back over his shoulder at her. Licking the end of her pencil, she said, "Sam. I think we'll name you Sam. You're a good secret keeper, just like that brother of mine was."

Tam cocked his head to one side.

"Do you like that name, *Sam*?"

Something pulled deep in Tam's heart.

CHAPTER 27

Abby

I sat next to Miss Bettis on the concrete steps, watching the kids standing around on the playground, not doing anything. They were all so busy texting and calling and listening to their own private music, nobody said word one to anyone else. And, of course, the Queen stood away from everybody in her black clothes, looking bored. It was downright ridiculous. Here it was, warm and sunny (for late January) and best of all, dry, and they all stood around like a bunch of antisocial sheep.

"I've had about all of this I can take." I handed Miss Bettis the map of the trip from Harmony Gap to Nashville I'd been working on and marched out to the playground.

I picked up a perfectly good ball. "Hey, everybody!" I hollered in my loudest voice.

Hardly anybody glanced my way. I tried again. No one batted an eye.

"Here, Abby," Miss Bettis called, holding out her special emergency whistle on a string.

I put that shiny whistle to my lips and blew with all my might. That got everybody's attention.

"Who wants to play dodgeball?" I asked, holding up the ball.

They all looked at me like I was speaking in some kind of foreign tongue.

I tossed the ball back and forth, from one hand to another. "Come on, y'all. Let's play. It'll be fun. That's what recess is for."

"I remember playing that in elementary school," Bree said, rolling her eyes and flipping her hair. "We're too old to play dodgeball."

Someone said, "Wasn't there a movie called *Dodgeball*?"

And another person said, "Yeah, it was pretty funny."

Then someone else said, "What'll I do with my cell phone?"

Miss Bettis spoke up. "Everyone bring your cell phones and iPods over to me. I'll take good care of them while you play." She winked at me.

Finally, I had enough kids to make two teams. At first,

they wanted to play boys against girls, but since most of the girls were in those skirts and boots, I decided to divide up the teams myself.

I drew a long line in the sand with the toe of my sneaker, and explained the rules. "Okay, each team takes a turn trying to hit someone on the other team with the ball. If a person gets hit, they have to go sit with Miss Bettis. The team getting the ball thrown at them can dodge the ball, but they can't cross this line. The first team to get all the players out, wins."

"And no hitting someone in the head with the ball," Miss Bettis called from the sidelines.

I threw out the first ball, and right away conked Billy Ray Purdee in the shoulder. "You got to *move* to avoid the ball, Billy Ray," I said. Billy Ray was kind of fat, so I decided to give him another chance. Pretty soon, everybody was getting into the spirit of things. The kids ran and laughed and yelled. It sounded like a real playground for the first time. Even Madison and some of the other girls had fun playing, once they stopped worrying so much about their hair.

When the bell rang, ending recess, everybody was kind of sad. Guys who'd never even said boo to each other slapped each other's backs and said, "Great shot," or "You couldn't hit the broad side of a barn." Courtney said, "Can we play again tomorrow, Abby?"

"Sure thing," I said. "I know all kinds of other games too."

Miss Bettis handed me back my map as we filed inside. "Good job, Abby," she said. And I don't think she was talking about my map.

The next day at recess, a whole bunch of kids wanted to play. They all gave Miss Bettis their cell phones and stuff as soon as we got outside. By the end of the week, I'd gotten them to play kickball, too. Even Bree.

I waited out front for Mama's car after school on Friday. A whole gaggle of girls waited with me.

"Abby, *please* come with us to see the new movie at the mall tomorrow," Courtney said. "It's supposed to be so cool."

"Yeah," Bree said. "I love the theme song from the movie they play all the time on WKDF."

I'd hardly ever gone to a big theater in a shopping mall. Olivia and I went to the Reel Time Theater in Harmony Gap. I was kind of curious. "I'll ask Mama," I said.

Just then, I heard a car horn blow. Mama waved from a line of cars. And right behind her truck was a shiny black limousine.

"Gotta go," I said.

"Call me tonight," Madison said.

I trotted out to Mama's truck. I was so busy looking to

see who would be picked up in a limo, I about ran smack into Cheyenne Rivers.

"Watch it, hillbilly," she growled.

"S-sorry," I stammered.

Then, just as it occurred to me she had called me the word I hated most, and I was about to tell her what a rude snot she was, she jerked open the back door of the limo and slid in.

Of course.

I hopped into Mama's truck and slammed the door.

Mama glanced in the rearview mirror. "Who was that?"

"That's that snotty ol' Cheyenne Rivers," I grumbled.

Mama shot me a look. "Watch your mouth, Abby."

"She about ran me over getting to her car, Mama, and then she called me 'hillbilly.'" Of all people, Mama knew how much I hated being called that.

Mama eased out into traffic. "One person being rude doesn't give you permission to be rude too."

I sighed. Mama would never understand.

Later that night, the phone rang. It was Madison. "Did you ask your mom about the movie?"

I'd totally forgotten. "I'll call you back in just a minute," I said.

Mama and Daddy sat at the kitchen table, going over bills. This never put them in the best mood.

"Mama," I said, "could I go to a movie tomorrow afternoon?"

"Who with?" Mama asked, not looking up.

"Just some girls from school," I said. "They want to see that new movie *Tennessee Home*."

"Sure, you can go," Mama said. She smiled at Daddy. "That'll give me and your dad some time to ourselves."

Daddy looked up from the mess of bills and smiled. "A few of the songs in that movie were recorded at our studio."

"Really?" I said. Boy, wait until I told Bree, Madison, and Courtney about that. They'd never think I wasn't cool again.

"Nothing but country bubblegum, if you ask me," Daddy said, laughing. "But some of the guys were real nice."

"But you might as well go too, Holly," Daddy said, rubbing the back of his neck, not looking at Mama. "I got to be at the studio most of the day tomorrow. Again."

I swear I saw tears in Mama's eyes. "But why?" she asked. "I thought you were done with the demo."

Daddy sighed. "Mr. Katz doesn't like most of our songs. He wants us to record a bunch of new ones, ones *he's* picked out."

Big ol' storm clouds gathered above Mama's eyes. It didn't take a weatherman to know thunder and lightning were on their way. I grabbed the phone, went back to my bedroom, and closed the door.

After I called Madison, I thought about emailing Olivia. But that meant going through the kitchen to get to Mama's office where the computer was, and I could still hear Mama and Daddy arguing.

So, instead, I picked up my guitar and strummed the opening chords of "The Wayfaring Stranger." I leaned my back against my pillows and sang:

> *I am a poor wayfaring stranger*
> *Wandering through this world of woe.*
> *Lookin' for no sickness, toil, or danger*
> *In that bright land to which I go.*
> *I'm goin' there to meet my mother.*
> *She said she'd meet me when I come.*
> *I'm only going over Jordan,*
> *I'm only going to my home.*

CHAPTER 28

Tam

As Tam grew stronger, as he lived again among the comforts and smells of humans, memories of another home flooded back. Memories of a farm in the green folds of the mountains to the south; of hands that were not this old woman's, stroking him and loving him; of nights in the safety of a warm, soft bed, the music of a voice whispering to him in the dark; the memory of a name that was not Sam, but almost.

Tam had been with Ivy a little over a month when she first noticed it. He gladly accompanied her on daily chores and walked the property when the weather was good. He was content to lie at her feet as she ate her lunch and read. But every afternoon, as the sun's shadows stretched long across the frozen ground, he grew restless.

He'd rise and trot to the door. He'd whine and look back at the old woman.

And every time, she would let him out. "Okay, Sam, go do your business."

But Tam just stood on the porch, looking bewildered. As if, Ivy thought, he'd entered a room but couldn't remember why.

After this occurred several days in a row, Ivy kept count of the time. Three fifteen, he'd rise, go to the front door, and whine. He'd jump up on the cedar chest beneath the tall living room window, jump down, and poke the door with his muzzle.

By three thirty, the pacing would start. Back and forth, back and forth, from door to window, something drove him.

And then, several minutes later, he would collapse at Ivy's feet with a groan of disappointment.

Ivy would lift him into her ample lap and stroke him until he slept.

Light from the fireplace glowed on Tam's deep red coat. Doc Pritchett appraised the dog stretched before the fireplace. "He's a sheltie, all right," he said. "Little on the small side, but a purebred, no doubt."

Ivy nodded and smiled. "Amazing what a little love, a

lot of food, and a bath will do. 'Course, modern medicine and a good doctor don't hurt either." They gazed at Tam in companionable silence; the only sound the fire crackling inside and the new storm outside.

Ivy sighed and shook her head. "I just don't know, though. . . ."

"What's troubling you?"

"He's as devoted a companion as I could ever wish for, just like you said he'd be. I couldn't imagine life without him."

"But?"

Her brow furrowed. "It just seems like his *heart* is somewhere else. Like a big part of him is looking for someone."

The old vet fell silent.

"I've even worried sometimes when I let him out at night to do his business that he might run off."

"Now, Ivy," he said, "where in the world would he run off *to*, especially in the dead of winter?"

"I know I sound like a silly old fool," she said, "but I just can't shake the feeling he was on his way to somewhere, on a journey." And then Ivy described Tam's afternoon ritual.

Doc Pritchett stretched his legs in front of him. Tam jumped to his feet and moved into the shadows. "Dogs are creatures of habit, Ivy. Who knows what's ingrained in that dog." The vet shook his head. "I still maintain whoever had him doesn't deserve him. You and I both know what terrible shape he was in. And even after all this time he still doesn't trust me; I'd wager doesn't even like me."

"James . . ."

He waved away his hurt. "All I'm saying is I strongly suspect this little dog was abused and neglected by a man. If he was on his way *to* somewhere, it was to a better home. And he found it with you."

Tam jumped into Ivy's lap. She stroked the top of his fine head, gazed into his brown eyes.

"Ivy, he's your dog now."

"Some famous poet said April is the cruelest month, but I think February is worse," Ivy said to Tam as they watched snow blow through the branches of the great pines. "Why, just last week, it was warm as a spring day." She sighed and turned away from the window and the storm beyond.

It had been snowing or sleeting for the last three days, turning the roads and the steps treacherous. "If I can't get out of this cabin soon," Ivy said, "I think I'll go stir-crazy."

Tam whined in sympathy.

Ivy smiled and scratched him behind his ear. "Oh, don't mind me, Sam. You'd think after living in these mountains over eighty years, I'd know about changeable weather by now." She picked up her knitting, brushed her fingers across the soft rows of llama fleece. "Still, it seems the older I get the longer winter is."

Tam ran his nose along the skein of llama wool in Ivy's lap. Pictures flashed in his mind of a barn filled with wooly, long-necked creatures. He saw a woman pitching hay and mixing grain. He sniffed the wool again. He smelled old apple orchards, wood smoke, a girl's sweet scent.

His heart filled. This was the scent of home.

Tam furrowed his brow, whined, and pawed Ivy's leg.

"What is it, Sam?"

The phone rang. "Why hello, Randall, honey. It's good to hear your voice." And this time Ivy meant it. She got up to fix herself a cup of tea, letting her son's deep voice warm her.

"Lord yes, honey," she said. "It's been snowing and blowing to beat the band. One minute it's sleeting and the next it switches over to snow." Tam watched her balance the phone against her ear as she lit the burner beneath the kettle.

Ivy took a dog biscuit out of a tin and handed it to Tam. "No, no, I don't dare go out. I expect the roads are sheets of ice. I worry about my birds, though. I haven't been able to feed them in days."

The kettle whistled. A strong memory swept through Tam. A memory of another kitchen and dinner next to a stove and the love he had for a girl.

"I think the weatherman said this storm is supposed to move on south by the end of the week. I sure hope so.

I'm about flat out of food." Ivy poured boiling water over the tea bag.

"Why yes, honey, I'd love to have you come visit this weekend. I could do with a little human company." Looking down apologetically at Tam, she said, "And I have a special friend I want you to meet."

"Thank the good Lord that weatherman was right for once," Ivy said, pulling on her boots. After two days, the storm had indeed moved on. Sun touched the tops of the trees on the far ridge for the first time in many days. Wrapping a scarf around her neck and stuffing the bag of bread crumbs in her coat pocket, Ivy said, "Come on, Sam. It's time to see those mountains come alive."

Snow crunched beneath Ivy's boots as they walked slowly along the fence line. She squinted her eyes against the bright glare of sun on snow. "Lovely," she murmured to Tam.

Leaning heavily on her walking stick, Ivy made her way down the gentle slope to the dogwood forest, Tam by her side. Chickadees flitted branch to branch, fluffing their feathers against the cold. The occasional flash of red announced the presence of a male cardinal or two. Ivy shook the bag of crumbs onto the snow. "Come here, my little babies," she called. "Come get your treats!" The notch-tailed raven called from the high branches of an old pine. "There's some for you too, old friend," Ivy said with a laugh.

Tam followed a scent down toward the riverbank. Delicate, heart-shaped tracks filled his nose with deer. Three had passed this way just forty-five minutes before, his nose told him. They were hungry. One was old and sick. His nose told him that too. A dog's keen sense of smell can read the story on earth and wind as clearly as any human can read a book.

Just as he began to stalk a snowshoe hare, Ivy called, "Sam! Sam! Come here, Sam!" The hare startled and ran. Tam sighed. He shook himself and trotted back up the bank to the old woman.

"Where'd you get to, boy?" Ivy said. "You gave me a little start."

Tam walked close by her side as they made their way back to the cabin. There was some indefinable scent on the woman that worried the little sheltie.

"I got to get on back and make up my grocery list before the boy gets here. Lord, I got to clean up those breakfast dishes too. Randall will think I've got the Alzheimer's if there's dishes in the sink. And I'm going to get him to put that identification tag on your collar."

Ivy stopped to catch her breath at the top of the pasture. She rubbed her shoulder. "Lord, Lord," she said. "I'm getting old." She gripped her walking stick and straightened her spine. "Nothing to do with age, Sam. Just been cooped up in that cabin too long. You and me got to get out more."

As Ivy opened the front door, it hit her like a freight train.

She doubled over in pain and dropped her stick. "Sweet Jesus," she gasped. Hot, searing pain shot up her arm, blazed across her chest. With steely determination, she straightened and pushed through the door. Out of habit, she pulled it closed behind her.

Her breath came in ragged gasps. Sweat poured down her face. Her world, the cabin, and all that she had known for more than eighty years fell away to one purpose: She must get to the telephone.

"Come on, old girl, you can do it," she said aloud. She clutched chair backs and countertops and worked her way to the telephone. Just as she stretched her hand out, an iron fist squeezed down hard on her heart. Her legs gave way. She crumpled forward, slamming her head on the floor.

Tam barked frantically. Everything was wrong. The scent of fear and sickness filled the air. The woman smelled of blood and pain. Tam pawed her outstretched hand. She groaned. He licked the blood from her face, sniffed her breath. "Sam," she breathed.

And then, all was silent. The clock ticked in the

hallway, water dripped from the faucet in the kitchen sink. The wind sighed in the trees. The raven called from somewhere outside the house. Tam lay next to the old woman and rested his head on her hip, his brown eyes abrim with sorrow.

After some time, Tam heard tires crunch up the drive to the house. He knew that sound. He ran to the cedar chest, jumped up, and barked at the big truck. A man stepped out, ran up the porch steps. Tam barked and barked. The man knocked once, left a package by the door, waved to Tam, and ran back to the truck.

Tam whined as the truck pulled away. He went back to the woman, sniffed her face. Her breath came in tattered threads. Her eyelids fluttered. Tam pawed the front of her coat. She opened her eyes. "Good boy," she said. And closed her eyes again.

More time passed. The slam of a car door woke Tam. He sat up and listened to the sound of heavy footsteps on the porch steps. A man. A big man. Tam growled low in his chest.

Ivy's son picked up the package the UPS driver left. He pushed open the door and stomped the snow off his boots. "Mama, you got a package," he called. Tam pushed closer into the woman's side and growled louder.

Randall dropped the package. "Mama?" he called. His eyes swept the room. The fire was out, dishes were piled beside the sink, the lights were off, and there was the sound of a dog growling. His instinct as a policeman took over. He reached back through the open door, grabbed a piece of firewood from the stack on the porch, and walked slowly toward the kitchen.

Fearful, sickening memories flooded Tam: a big man with a long stick in his hand coming toward him. Tam stood beside the crumpled figure on the floor, eyes wide with fear, teeth bared to protect his friend. He growled a warning to the man to go away.

"Oh good Lord," Randall said at the sight of his mother on the floor, blood on her face, this dog crouched over her. Randall raised the piece of wood, brandishing it like a club. "Get out of here!" he yelled.

Tam barked and snapped. Randall started to swing the club down on Tam, then realized he risked hitting his mother too. Instead, he rushed Tam, yelling, pretending to swing.

Tam bolted past the man into the living room. He whirled and barked furiously. The man threw the piece of wood at Tam, catching the side of his head. Tam yelped in pain. Still he would not leave his friend. He took a step forward and barked the gruffest bark he could muster.

When the man grabbed a plate from the counter and hurled it, Tam finally fled out the front door and into the woods.

He circled back and watched the house from the cover of the laurel thicket. He heard the man's voice, fear-filled, inside the house. He heard the old woman's voice faint as a spider's web. He watched as the big man carried her to his car, laid her gently in the backseat, and drove away.

Nightfall came. The air turned from cold to freezing. The man had not closed the door when he had carried Ivy to his car. Tam poked his head around the door and listened. Quiet.

Tam ate the last of his dry kibble and drank deeply from the water dish. He sniffed the chair by the fireplace where the woman sat at night. His toenails clicked on the pine floors as he trotted from room to room looking for any signs of the old woman. There were none. He sniffed the square brown package on the floor. If Tam could've read, he'd have known the label said *Whistler Farm Specialty Fibers.*

He trotted up the stairs to her bedroom and jumped up on the bed. He found a lingering scent of her on the pillow and lay down. But he could not sleep. For the first time, the scent of the old woman felt wrong. He should have been surrounded by the scent of a girl. His girl.

CHAPTER 29

Abby

To: omcbuttars@carolinanet.com
From: "Abby Whistler" <sheltiegirl@carolinanet.com>
Date: Sunday, February 21 11:03 am
Subject: Hey again

Hey Olivia,

I just talked to Meemaw a little bit ago. She said it was snowing to beat the band. Said she hasn't seen such a snowy winter in a long time. She sure does appreciate all you and your grandpa are doing for her.

Maybe you're right. Maybe I haven't dreamed about Tam because he's doing okay. He's safe. At least I hope so. Or maybe you were wrong about me having the Sight like Meemaw.

Not much going on here to speak of. This is Mama's weekend to work. Working a weekend sure does make her grumpy. She was in such a bad mood this morning, I said, "Mama, who peed on your Cheerios?" Usually when I say that to her, it at least makes her smile. But not this morning.

Daddy's been on the phone all blessed morning with his boss and the guys in his band, setting everything up for the big tour they're going on. I was hoping me and him could do something together today, just the two of us, like old times. But he just waved me away and said, "Not now, peanut." Just when IS "not now"? That's what I want to know.

I could have gone to the mall with some of the girls from school. They want to shop for clothes and makeup. I'd rather sort lint than shop for clothes. Anybody who knows Abby Whistler knows that. Sometimes I'm not sure who the girl is Madison and Bree think they know.

Your friend,

Abby (who hates shopping and always will)

"Daddy," I said, planting myself right in front of him and that telephone, "I'm going for a walk."

Daddy's wild red hair shot off in twenty different directions, looking like it was in full agreement about how crazy everything was.

Daddy nodded and put his hand over the mouthpiece of the phone. "Have a good time, sugar."

As I pulled on my coat, I heard him say to the person on the phone, "No, sir, I wasn't calling you sugar. I was just . . ."

Poor Daddy.

I headed down the sidewalk past the little houses on our street. They were all tiny and hunched together like a bunch of wet chickens in the cold. I hardly ever saw kids playing out in the little-bitty yards or riding their bikes. I reckon they were all inside watching TV or playing video games or out shopping at the mall.

I turned on Edge Hill and cut over to Music Row. I liked that area for all its trees and colorful houses. I saw all kinds of people walking along with guitar cases and such strapped to their backs. I reckon they were all following their north star, just like Daddy.

Thinking of Daddy and his north star made me think of Tam, my north star. My heart got all heavy and sad.

Actually, ever since I'd seen that movie *Tennessee Home*, I'd been kind of down in the dumps. When that girl was sent from the city to live with her family at their home way out in the country, it made me miss my home in the mountains. She didn't have the great big mountains like I did, but she had lots and lots of green grass under her feet instead of this concrete, and big fields and pastures full of flowers, just like home. I swear, the whole movie I kept expecting to see a red and white sheltie come running across the fields, grinning his sheltie grin.

A horn honked, and then another. I stopped and looked around. I'd been thinking so hard about Tam and Wild Cat Cove, I hadn't realized where I was.

I turned all around and looked. Traffic and people were hurrying every which way. Big, tall buildings climbed up and up. I craned my neck till it about broke off to see the sky. Everywhere I looked there were people, buildings, and cars. In all my thinking, I'd walked smack into downtown Nashville.

I took a deep breath to calm my hammering heart. I pointed my toes in front of me and followed them down the street. Just about every store I passed had music coming out of it. That and the smell of food. My stomach grumbled.

I was just about to turn around and find my way home when I spotted a big river. It'd been so long since I'd seen a river or creek or anything, I just had to go pay my respects.

I trotted down to the end of the sidewalk and crossed First Avenue. I leaned against the railing and drank in the sight of that big ol' river lumbering along. I closed my eyes and listened for its voice. I knew, even right smack-dab in the middle of this big city, the river would have a voice— just like Clear Creek and the apple trees in our orchard and the big willow down by the creek. I held my breath and listened real hard.

A crow cawed. A boat horn honked. And then . . .

"Oh no!"

My eyes flew open. This was not what I expected to hear the river say.

I heard car tires squeal and even more horns honking than usual.

I turned around to see what all the ruckus was about.

Right there on the sidewalk, hardly ten feet away, a girl jumped up and down, screaming and waving.

"Please!" she hollered. "Don't hit my dog!"

Dog?

And sure enough, there it was, a tiny little bit of a thing dashing in and out of traffic.

The girl darted into traffic too, yelling, "Dusty! Come here, Dusty!" A car swerved to one side, just barely missing the girl. Still, Dusty did what every dog does when someone chases after him: He ran away.

"Great bucket of gravy!" I dashed over and called to the girl, "His name's Dusty?"

She looked over at me. Her face was streaked with tears underneath the bill of her purple baseball cap. "Yes," she sobbed.

I looked up the street. The cars at the traffic light were just leaving. I looked down the street. Those cars were still waiting for the light to turn.

And that crazy little dog, no bigger than a dust bunny, stood right in the middle of that street.

I grabbed the girl's arm. I had no doubt what was running through her head. "*Don't* chase him," I commanded.

I took one little step toward the dog and whistled. He looked at me and cocked his head to one side.

The cars from up the street were coming closer.

I swallowed hard and pitched my voice as high and as excited as I could. I clapped my hands and called, "Here, Dusty! Come see what I got!"

He took one little step toward me, just the tip of his tail wagging.

The cars were almost upon us.

I clapped and called to him again. "Oh, look here, Dusty! Isn't this fun?"

And then I took little baby steps, running away from him, clapping and calling, "Come come come, Dusty! Come come come!"

Now, anybody who knows squat about dogs knows they can't resist an excited voice and a good game of chase.

Dusty dashed right after me, yapping his fool little head off about a mile a nanosecond. It was, quite frankly, an annoying yap. But I didn't care. He'd followed me out of the street, across the plaza, and over to the grass.

I knelt on the ground and got down as low as I could. "Come here, you little mouse," I said, laughing. He jumped in my lap and covered my face with kisses as fast as his little pink tongue would go. I couldn't believe how good it felt to have a dog kissing me again.

"Oh my God, I can't believe you rescued him."

I squinted up into the sun. For just a split second, I'd kind of forgotten all about him being someone else's dog.

I scooped up the little pup with one hand and stood. I brushed my hair, which had gone all scatter-wonky, out of my face, and handed her the dog. "Here you go. I don't think he's any worse for wear."

The pup was surely excited to see his girl. He licked her face and tried to climb up her neck.

We both laughed. "He sure is an excitable little guy, isn't he?" I said. The dog about knocked her hat off her head.

I froze. I gasped.

She opened those ice blue eyes of hers and stared down at me.

"It's *you*," we both said at the exact same moment.

It was the Queen, Cheyenne Rivers, looking right down her nose at me like I'd dropped out of the sky from an alien spaceship.

But it wasn't the Cheyenne Rivers I knew either. Instead of her usual black clothes, she wore an old jacket and jeans. Instead of those big army boots with all those buckles, she had on just a regular pair of sneakers. Her face was scrubbed clean of makeup and her ponytail stuck through the back of her baseball cap. I couldn't believe it. She looked like a regular kid.

She hugged her little Dusty against her chest and looked away. I figured she was about to tell me to scram, tell me to get out of her city.

But do you know what? She buried her face in that little dog's side and said in a voice I could barely hear, "Thank you so much."

Well, that about shocked the socks off me. But then she did an even more shocking thing. She started to cry.

Now, if anybody'd told me the Queen was capable of shedding one tear, I would've told them maybe pigs could fly too. But there she was, crying all over her dog.

I touched her arm. "He's okay, Cheyenne. Really."

Dusty licked at the tears coming down her cheeks, just like Tam used to.

"I don't know what I would have done if he'd gotten hurt," she sobbed.

Squashed like a bug on a windshield more likely, but I didn't say that. Instead, I just stood close and patted her arm.

Finally, she scrubbed her sleeve across her face and looked at me. I tried out a smile on her. She laughed.

I took a step back and got ready for whatever insults she was going to throw at me. Instead she said, "Anybody'd think we called each other this morning."

I shook my head. I had no idea what she was talking about.

With her free hand, she motioned to my jeans, my shoes. "We're dressed just alike," she said chuckling.

And do you know what? She was right! Jeans, old flannel shirts, ratty jackets, and sneakers.

I laughed and pointed. "You look like a hillbilly!"

Her face turned red. "Sorry about that. I didn't really mean it in a bad way."

I smiled. "That's okay. In my head, I call you the Queen."

She let out a big belly laugh. "Oh my gosh, that's what I call my *mother*."

It was pretty funny.

"Do you live around here?" she asked.

"No," I said. "I live over by Music Row. I got bored and decided to go for a walk and—" I looked around at the river and tall buildings. "Here I am."

"Wow," she said. "That's kind of a long walk, isn't it?"

I shrugged. "What about you?" I asked. "Do you and Dusty live around here?"

She sighed. "No, we live out in Belle Meade." When I shrugged, she said, "It's kind of a long ways from here. I got bored too, though."

"You walked too?" I asked.

She shook her head. "Took the bus."

My eyes popped open. "They let dogs on the bus here?"

She laughed and pointed to the big canvas bag on the ground. "Dusty rode in that."

I'd seen pictures in magazines of famous movie stars and such carrying their little dogs in purses. "Wow, you've got a dog purse."

"Yep," she said. "That way, he can go with me just about everywhere." She stroked the little dog's ears. "He's my best friend."

I nodded. I knew just how that was. All of a sudden, I found myself liking Cheyenne Rivers.

She dug around in that big canvas sack and pulled out a soda. "Want it?" She held the can out to me.

"That's okay," I said. "I'm not allowed to drink Cokes. My mama says they'll eat the enamel off my teeth."

She put a hand on her hip and cocked her head. "Do you see your mama around here?"

I laughed and took the can. She took another one out of that bag and popped the top. She also pulled out a bag of Cheetos, the crispy kind, which are my favorite. And then—I couldn't believe it—she pulled a tiny little dish and a water bottle out of that bottomless bag and poured Dusty a drink!

We sat on the grass enjoying our Cokes and Cheetos, not saying much. But it was a good not-saying-much, a comfortable, smiling together not-saying-much.

And then it started to rain. It was like someone flipped a switch and the rain came pouring down.

We gathered up all our stuff and ran to a shelter by the river. Cheyenne watched the rain and said, "So much for Camelot."

"Excuse me?"

"Camelot," she repeated. "You know, the perfect place where King Arthur and Sir Lancelot and Guinevere lived?"

I nodded. "I think my friend Olivia told me about that place."

She rooted around in her bag again and pulled out a red, sparkly cell phone. "Let's go to my house," she said.

She punched some numbers into her phone. "Hi, Richard, it's me. Can you come pick me up?" She smiled. "And a friend too. We're down at Riverfront Park across from First Avenue."

She snapped her cell phone shut. "He'll be here in a few minutes."

"Is Richard your brother or something?" I asked.

"No," she said. "My driver."

As the long black limousine purred down the interstate, I tried to act like I rode in limos all the time. I tried not to gawk too much at the TVs and tiny refrigerator and computer. There were all kinds of secret cabinets and drawers. I about wet my pants.

We pulled into a huge, semicircular driveway. Richard opened the door for us.

"Thanks a lot," I said. "You drive real good."

We went up about a million marble stairs. A woman in an apron opened the biggest doors I've ever seen. I figured it was Cheyenne's mama.

Wrong again. "Welcome back, Miss Rivers," the woman said in an annoyed kind of way.

"Thanks, Eudora," Cheyenne said. "We're hungry. Could you fix my friend and me some sandwiches and bring them up to my room?"

And without even waiting for an answer, Cheyenne said, "My room's up here, Abby."

Let me tell you, that whole upstairs of their house could have held our entire house in Wild Cat Cove. I've never seen so many hallways and doors leading to lord knows where. Seemed like every other door, she'd point and say, "There's a bathroom if you need it."

Loud *thump, thump, thump*ing came from behind one door. If the carpet hadn't been so thick, you could have felt the floor vibrating beneath your feet. Cheyenne pushed open the door and yelled, "Hey, Harley." The music coming from the room about knocked me backward.

A big, tall boy turned from the computer on his desk. "What's up?"

Cheyenne pushed me forward. "This is my friend

195

Abby. Abby, this is my brother, Harley."

Harley bobbed his head in my general direction. "Cool."

"Hey," I said.

"Where's the Momster?" Cheyenne asked.

"At the club, where she usually is," Harley said.

Cheyenne rolled her eyes. "Totally."

"Totally," Harley agreed, and turned back to his computer.

Cheyenne led me down the hall to the last closed door. She pulled it open, and I stepped into another universe. Cheyenne didn't seem to think there was anything unusual about the fact that she had not only a bathroom in her bedroom, but a small kitchen and fireplace! Her bed sat in the middle of the huge room like an island amid a sea of clothes strewn across the floor.

But once I got used to her room, I felt like I was with Olivia in her room. We sprawled across her bed and talked and talked and talked. She told me how much she hated living in the city, how much she missed the farm they'd lived on in Leipers Fork.

"Hey," I said, "isn't that where some of that *Tennessee Home* movie was filmed?"

She rolled her eyes again. "You saw that?"

I shrugged.

"Yeah," she said. "That's the place. We have an old

farmhouse and about sixty acres out there. I even have a couple of horses."

"Why'd you move to town?" I asked.

"My mom hates the country. Too far from shopping and the country club. She doesn't even like going out there on the weekends."

I told her all about our place in Wild Cat Cove, about the apple orchard and Lake Inferior and the llamas, about Clear Creek and the willow tree.

We were both quiet for a while, then she said, "How come you know so much about dogs?"

I really hadn't planned on it, but the whole blessed story of Tam just came pouring out. And do you know what? She listened, really listened.

"I know it sounds crazy and all, but I just can't shake the feeling he's coming home," I said. "That's a big part of why I was so upset when we had to move here."

Cheyenne shook her head. "I don't think it's crazy. Haven't you ever read *Lassie Come-Home* or *The Incredible Journey*?"

Before I could answer, she jumped off her bed and went to one of her many bookcases. I thought Olivia had a lot of books, but Cheyenne had enough books to practically fill the Balsam County Library at home.

She tossed two books onto the bed. "Take them home with you. I've read them a million times at least."

I glanced at the clock on her wall.

"Holy moley, I got to get home," I said.

The tires of the black limo hissed on the rain-wet streets as we eased down my street. Mama's truck was in the driveway.

"I had a real good time today," I said to Cheyenne.

She smiled. "Mutual." She held Dusty to my cheek. "Kiss Abby good-bye," she cooed. Dusty gave my cheek a dainty little lick.

"Bye, Mr. Richard, thanks again," I said.

Mr. Richard touched the edge of his cap. "You're most welcome, Miss Abby."

I ran up the walkway, jumped up onto our saggy little porch, and burst in the front door. I heard Mama and Daddy's voices in the kitchen. "Hey," I called. "You'll never guess what!"

Mama raced out of the kitchen and locked me up in such a ferocious hug, she about broke my ribs.

She held me away from her. Her face was red and wet. "Thank the Lord, you're okay!"

I glanced from her to Daddy, standing in the doorway looking like a whipped puppy. "Of course I'm okay. Why wouldn't I be?"

"Where in the world have you been?" Mama asked. "I've been crazy with worry!"

"I went for a walk," I said. "I told Daddy."

"That was hours ago, peanut," Daddy said.

"Oh, well, I walked and walked and do you know the next thing I knew I was right in downtown Nashville, and then there was this girl hollering for help because her little-bitty dog had gotten loose and was about to get squashed out in traffic, so I—"

Mama whirled on Daddy like some crazy person. "See? What did I tell you, Ian?"

Daddy held his hands up like he was fending off a rabid dog. "Now, Holly, she's okay, isn't she?"

"Mama," I said, tugging on her sleeve, "let me tell you the rest of what happened. I'm just getting to the really *good* part."

Ignoring me, Mama said, "Don't you get it? This is *not* home! It's one thing in Wild Cat Cove or even Harmony Gap to let Abby go off on her own exploring all day. But not here!"

"But Mama . . ."

Mama glared at me. "Go to your room now, Abigail Andrea Whistler," she snapped.

Later that night, Mama came into my room. "Can I come in, Abby?"

I set aside *Lassie Come-Home*. "If you're done yelling at me."

Mama sniffed and wiped at her eyes. "I'm sorry, honey," she said. "I was scared."

She climbed in beside me on my bed. She wrapped me in her arms—something she hadn't done in a long time—rocked me just a tiny bit. I listened to the *thump thump* of her heart.

Finally she said, "Tell me the rest of the story about your day, Abby," and I did. I told her all about riding in the limousine and how Cheyenne's house not only had big white pillars on the outside, but on the inside too. "And do you know what, Mama? Cheyenne even has a little kitchen in her bedroom, and a bathroom, *and* a fireplace too!"

"Good gravy," Mama said.

Then I told her about all the things Cheyenne and I have in common and how she misses her home in the country too. "You sure can never tell about folks, can you, Mama?"

CHAPTER 30

Tam

A car door slammed; the faint sound of voices. Tam raised his head from the icy river and cocked his ears toward the house.

He worked his way up from the riverbank through the new snow. Maybe the old woman was back and she would feed him dinner, stroke his head. Two days had passed since she left, and all the kibble was gone.

He heard that name that was almost his name but not quite. "Sam!" floated down through the woods from the cabin. Tam stopped at the edge of the woods. It was not her voice.

Doc Pritchett cupped his hands around his mouth and called again. "Sam! Come here, Sam!"

Randall ran his hand through his black hair. "How the heck was I supposed to know she had a dog? She never told me she had a dog. I'd sure never seen one."

"And when was the last time you actually visited your mama?" Doc Pritchett said.

Randall shrugged. "A couple weeks before Christmas, I guess. For a day or two."

The vet didn't say anything, just studied the front yard.

Randall pointed to the tracks on the porch. "Looks like he's been here, though. Maybe he's just out sniffing around, chasing a rabbit or something."

The vet shook his head. "He's a sheltie, not a hound. Shelties don't hunt." He squinted at the tracks in the snow. "If he's close by, why doesn't he come? Lord, your mama's going to pitch a fit if we don't find that little dog. She's gotten real attached."

Tam watched the two men on the porch. If it were just the old man, he'd have shown himself.

But the tall, dark man was there too. The one who had yelled at him and hurt him. As hungry and lonely as he was, Tam would not show himself to that man. Ever. He turned and followed his own tracks back down to the river.

As dusk stretched across the meadow, Tam went back to the cabin. The car was gone. No sound came from inside the house. The scent of the two men was faint.

And the front door, closed.

Tam barked once. This was what he had done at another home—a big white house at the top of a hill—when he was ready to come in. Someone always came. This time, no one did. Tam barked again, louder. Then he scratched at the door, something that always brought the words, "No, Tam!" But the door would open for him anyway. Not this time.

Tam trotted down the steps and around to the back of the house. Sometimes the old woman came and went from that door. It was closed too, and no amount of barking and scratching opened it.

Tam went back around to the front of the cabin. He had lived there for more than two months. She had always been there. Food and warmth had always been there. Now the cabin was silent. No smoke spiraled up from the chimney; no light in the windows.

He lay on the mat in front of the door with his bewilderment. He licked his paws over and over, a distraction from the hunger gnawing at his belly. He watched a barn owl hunting low over the far fields. A fox barked. Cold wind blew. Tam whimpered and curled up tight, nose buried under his tail.

The next morning when he awoke, he shook himself and stretched. Still, the fine web of his night's dream clung to him and burrowed in his heart—a dream of watching a sweeping meadow from the edge of a porch; hearing the music of a girl's—*his* girl's—voice calling, "Tam! Come here, Tam!" the voice lifting him, carrying him to the safety of her arms.

He trotted down the porch steps and stood in the front yard. His wet black nose worked back and forth. The wind from the south held a certain sweetness. He took two tentative steps toward the cabin and stood in indecision. Tam whined.

Then another sense rose in him—the homing sense. It pulled on him like the needle on a compass. He looked back at the cabin. There was nothing there to hold him. Home was not this place with the old woman; home was not at the side of his coyote friend. Home was his girl. He belonged with her.

He shook himself again. Like a traveler waking from a long dream, he struck out and resumed his journey south.

Tam followed the New River as it ran south and west of the old woman's home. The hard freezes at night kept the top crust of the snow firm enough for Tam to walk easily on it. He set a steady pace, covering many miles.

On the third day, Tam hesitated. The river turned abruptly north. He followed it for two or three miles, then stopped. This going did not feel right. The farther north he went, the more his compass told him to turn back.

He came across the remains of a deer carcass. Foxes, coyotes, and bobcats had stripped most of the meat. Tam hadn't eaten for three days. He managed to work loose a few strips of meat and skin.

Tam drank from the river, then napped in the pocket of the roots of a fallen birch.

The next morning, he left the New River and struck out south. By evening of the next day, Tam crossed the invisible line from Virginia into North Carolina. He had no way of knowing that. He had no way of knowing he had more than two hundred forty miles behind him, and that the mountains would now rise higher, the forests would now become wilder.

What Tam did know was that the wind had shifted direction. The air smelled wet and sharp and urgent. By late afternoon, thick gray clouds piled against the tops of the mountains and ridgelines. Late that night, as Tam slept tucked up tight under a rocky outcropping on a high ridge, a storm roared in from the north. Great gusts of wind-driven snow curtained the ridgetop.

When he woke the next morning, a light blanket of snow covered his body. Weak light filtered into his make-shift den. A thick wall of snow sealed closed the opening from the night before.

Tam pushed against the snow with his long muzzle. The wind had packed the snow as hard as concrete. Tam scratched at the snow wall with one paw. His claws barely left a trace.

Tam barked, then listened. The only sound was the beat of panic in his chest.

Then Tam heard a faint call from the laurel cove beneath the craggy rocks. He stopped panting and cocked his head to listen. The music of a coyote's howl drifted across the cove and up the rocky slope to Tam's white prison.

Tam barked in reply. The howl came again. He cocked his head to one side. Was it closer this time?

Tam clawed furiously at the wall of snow. His efforts made little difference.

He found a weaker spot in the wall. He felt a slight give beneath his paws. He clawed all the harder. Blood stained the white snow. His feet had grown soft during his months with the old woman. His shoulder ached.

He stopped and listened. Silence. He barked a high, seeking bark. Again, he heard the answer from below.

Feet bleeding, pain shooting through his shoulder, Tam broke through the white wall and into the sunlight. He fell onto the wind-packed snow, panting and blinking against the bright light. He licked the blood from his cut pads. One nail was torn away. He studied the snowbound forest for the coyote. He saw nothing. He barked once, then listened. His only answer was the caw of a raven.

He limped down the hillside to the laurel cove, his bloody footprints leaving a trail behind. If he could only find the coyote, he would be fine.

But there were no tracks of her. There was no musky smell of her, either. There were only the tracks of small birds, squirrels, and chipmunks.

Tam barked and listened. Then barked again. And again and again. At first he thought he heard her, but it was only his own voice echoing in reply. The coyote was not there. Tam threw back his head and howled his loneliness to the sky.

CHAPTER 31

Abby

"So anyway," Madison said, as if the sun rose and set by the latest school gossip, "I heard that Robert Lee asked Savannah Stiles to go to the seventh-grade spring dance!" Bree and Courtney gasped.

I glanced toward the cafeteria door, wishing Cheyenne would hurry up and get here. "What's so bad about him asking her?"

They all exchanged their Abby-is-so-clueless look. "He was supposed to ask Kristen Pettigrew."

Courtney nodded. "Yeah, everybody knows that."

Finally, Cheyenne strode into the cafeteria. Her eyes found me at the table with the others. She raised one eyebrow and nodded over to the window.

I wadded up my paper sack and stood. "I'll see y'all out at recess."

And just like every other day since Cheyenne and I had become friends, they looked on in disbelief as the little hillbilly went and ate lunch with the coolest girl in eighth grade, not to mention the whole school.

Cheyenne picked at her salad and fruit. Cheyenne Rivers was a vegetarian. She says she doesn't eat anything with a face. I had read about vegetarians before, but until I met Cheyenne, I'd never seen one.

"So what book does Olivia say we should read for our book club?" Cheyenne asked.

"She liked your suggestions best. She votes for *To Kill a Mockingbird*," I said.

Cheyenne smiled. "Good. I've read it a bunch of times, but I think you'll like it. You and Scout have a lot in common."

I'd told Cheyenne all about Olivia and me reading the same books together. Cheyenne thought that was a great idea, and now the three of us had our own online book club.

"They made a movie of it too," Cheyenne said. "I have it at home. We can watch it when we're done with the book."

The sun coming in the cafeteria windows tickled my hair and shoulders. It was the first sun we'd had all week.

I was itching to get outside at recess.

"How come you don't ever play kickball or four-square with us at recess?" I asked. "Other eighth graders do." Our games at recess had gotten so popular, practically everybody played.

Cheyenne shrugged. A little bit of red crept up her face. "Why should I care about a stupid game?"

So you can bet, that afternoon, when I picked my team for dodgeball, I pointed at Cheyenne over to the side, leaning against a tree like she didn't care a thing in the world. "I pick Cheyenne Rivers," I said real loud.

I'm here to tell you, you could've heard a pin drop on that playground. Half the kids looked at me like I was crazy, the other half watched Cheyenne to see what she'd do.

I was just as surprised as everyone else when she yawned, pushed herself off that tree, and said, "Sure, whatever."

At first, everybody on my team stayed way out of her way, and nobody on the other team tried to hit her with the ball.

I blew Miss Bettis's shiny silver whistle and called a time-out. "Kyle," I said, pointing to a seventh grader. "You and I are swapping sides."

I blew the whistle again, grabbed the ball, and took solid aim. It was time to show them that Cheyenne Rivers was just like everybody else.

* * *

That night at supper (Harris Teeter fried chicken again, I am sorry to say), Mama said, "Your daddy's going to be gone six weeks on this tour with the band, so I'm going to need extra help from you." Mama twisted and untwisted her long braid around her fingers like she does when she's extra unhappy with the world.

"Sure, Mama," I said. "It's not like he's around that much anyway."

Mama's face went white and her eyes got big as cat heads. Once again, I'd managed to stick my foot in my mouth.

"Oh my stars," Mama breathed.

I turned around to see what she was looking at. "Great bucket of gravy," I said.

There, in the living room, stood my daddy. At least, I think it was my daddy. Gone was the long, wild hair that had a life of its own; gone was the big red and silver beard he used to tickle my face. His hair was all short and slicked back. It looked like it'd never have a thought of its own again. And instead of his usual patched-up jeans or overalls, he wore fancy-stitched black pants, a cowboy shirt all tucked in, and a belt with a silver buckle as big as a hubcap.

My daddy had had a makeover.

"Ian," my mother whispered, her hand covering her

mouth, "what happened to you?"

Daddy stuck his hands in the pockets of his fancy pants and stared down at his pointy-toed boots. "Mr. Katz," he mumbled. "He said we have to project a 'Nashville image' when we go out on tour. Not a Harmony Gap image."

"Did you all have makeovers, Daddy?" I asked. Daddy winced and got all red in the face. Mama snorted behind her hand.

"Yes, sugar." Daddy sighed. "We all did. Cue Ball and the Stuarts were not too happy, I can tell you."

I cocked my head and studied Daddy. He looked an awful lot like Cheyenne's daddy. I'd seen pictures of him at her house.

I went and gave Daddy a big hug around his middle. "Don't feel too bad about it, Daddy. Mr. Randy Rivers dresses just like that and he's a millionaire."

Daddy smiled down at me and smoothed the top of my head. "Thanks, peanut. Right now, though, I think I'd pay a million dollars to get my hair back. My neck is darned cold."

The night before he left, Daddy came into my room. I was snuggled under my quilt reading.

He sat on the edge of the bed and tapped the back of my book. "*To Kill a Mockingbird*, huh? That's one of your Meemaw's favorite books."

"Me and Olivia and Cheyenne Rivers are reading it for our online book club. Cheyenne said I'd like it because of Scout and me being a lot alike."

Daddy laughed. "From what I remember about the story, I'd say she's right."

Daddy picked at a thread in Meemaw's quilt. "I'm sorry I have to be gone so long, Abby."

And do you know what? He sounded like he really was sorry.

"That's okay, Daddy," I said. "You got to follow your north star, right?"

Daddy kind of laughed, but his eyes didn't. "I want you to look after your mama for me. She's not real happy about this."

"But you've been on the road before," I pointed out.

"Yeah, but she always had her llamas before to keep her busy and Meemaw to help out. This is different. It's just going to be the two of you."

I swallowed hard. I hadn't thought about that. It was a fact Mama loved those llamas more than just about anything.

He patted my cheek and smiled. "Don't worry, though. I'll call a bunch and send postcards. March will fly by and I'll be back before you even have time to miss me."

I missed Daddy already. "I wish we could go with you," I said. "Like old times."

He pulled me to him. "Me too, honey. But just remember: Every night I'll be looking at that same big ol' moon as you and your mama are."

I almost pointed out that it's hard to see the moon in the city, but I didn't. "I'll try to remember," I said.

The next morning, after Daddy loaded the last of the instruments into his van, he grabbed me and Mama up in his strong arms and hugged us tight. "I will miss you girls more than you can ever know."

Mama started to say something, then buried her face in his old canvas jacket. He tipped my face up and said, "Don't forget what I told you about the moon, Abby."

"I won't, Daddy," I said around a lump in my throat the size of China.

He kissed Mama for a long time, and then he was gone.

Mama wandered around the house the rest of the day like she needed a map to figure out where she was. She'd start one thing, then put it down. She sat and stared at her computer screen but didn't type a single thing. Finally, I said, "Mama, let's go to the Swishy Washy."

The Swishy Washy was the Laundromat where we did the laundry every week. Mama maintained it was hard to feel bad when you said a name like Swishy Washy.

Mama stared out at the rain falling at the edge of our tiny porch. "I wonder if it's snowing at your grandmother's?" she said. "I hope the llamas are getting enough to eat."

I went over and stood next to Mama, resting my hand on her shoulder. "Come on, Mama," I said. "Let's get out of this house."

SPRING

CHAPTER 32

Tam

As the days passed, the wind shifted south, bringing the warmth from valleys four thousand feet below. Snow fell from burdened branches. The air filled with birdsong. Squirrels ran across the snow, tree to tree. Despite the frequent storms, the very fingertips of March touched the high mountains. The days were longer now, the sunlight stronger.

Every fiber of Tam's being wanted to be home. Spring meant time outdoors with the girl after long days indoors during the winter. Spring meant exploring along Clear Creek as the snow receded, revealing a symphony of new smells. Spring was waiting in a warm patch of sun on the front porch for his girl to come home from school. Time, the time was near for his girl. The fever of spring with the girl drove Tam beyond exhaustion and hunger. His heart ached for his girl.

As Tam rounded a sharp curve in the road, he startled a large snowshoe hare nibbling the tiny green shoots of grass at the edge of the road. The hare froze at the sight of the dog, then bolted.

Tam shot forward. In two swift pounces, he grabbed the back paw of the hare. The sweet taste of blood filled his mouth.

Just as Tam was about to pin the hare with his front leg, a huge, feathered form streaked down from the sky. The bald eagle struck at the front of the rabbit. The bird beat his wide wings, lifting his prize upward.

Tam did not let go. This was his kill. He grabbed the meaty thigh of the hare and jerked back.

The eagle screamed in outrage, beat his wings harder.

Tam sank all his weight onto his back legs and shook his head back and forth. The tip of a wing raked Tam's face. He squeezed his eyes closed and pulled back harder.

The eagle screamed its frustration again and beat its wing across the bridge of Tam's muzzle. Pain exploded in his head.

The eagle released the rabbit, then rose above Tam and dove downward, talons outstretched.

Tam's eyes widened as the huge bird fell upon him. Razor-sharp talons raked his back, his hip. The force of the eagle's blow rolled him end over end. The precious rabbit slipped from his mouth.

The eagle spotted the rabbit just beyond Tam's reach. He hopped and flapped toward the dog's kill.

But hunger quickened Tam's instincts. With a snarl, he charged the bird. He grabbed the hare around the middle and dashed for the deep forest, where the eagle could not follow.

With one last cry of outrage, the eagle rose above the forest and drifted away.

Tam hauled the dead rabbit up onto a large flat-topped boulder and collapsed in exhaustion and pain. He licked the oozing blood from the furrows left on his hip by the eagle. Then he turned his attention to his first meal in days.

As the sun rose high above the sea of gray mountains, Tam slept on the sun-warmed boulder. Bits of fluff and blood clung to his front paws and the edges of his mouth. Bloodstained snow and scattered bones were all the evidence left that the hare had ever lived.

A week later, spring fled the high mountains. A wild storm chased down from the north, roared across the high peaks and ridges, catching life unaware.

Tam had sensed a change coming the day before and had quickened his pace. Still, there was no predicting the crack of thunder, the plummeting temperatures. Snow swept across the high country and the far ridges in thick curtains of white.

Tam left the open road and sought shelter in the forest. Ice and snow stung his eyes. His face turned white. The swirling storm bent trees low and stripped limbs.

A half mile off the downhill side of the Parkway, Tam found shelter in an old shed. The door was long since missing, one corner of the tin roof torn away. But inside it was dry.

He scratched out a bed among dried corn husks and feed sacks. He laid his head across his tired paws and watched the storm through the open doorway. Thunder bounced from one side of the range to the other. Tam squeezed his eyes closed and whimpered.

Tam had never understood the electric flashes that split the sky, the booming thunder that shook the earth beneath his feet. It was everywhere and nowhere. But the girl had always kept him safe until the thing went away.

As lightning lit the silvered winter woods and thunder cracked overhead, Tam burrowed as far beneath the feed sacks as he could, reduced to a trembling ball. The dog who had faced down bear, shotgun, and eagle, whose brave, loyal heart had carried him hundreds of miles in winter wilderness, cowered before the unseen, alone.

* * *

Seventy-four miles to the north, Ian Whistler stood in the Galax, Virginia, post office, watching the unexpected storm beyond the glass doors. He had just mailed the postcard he'd written to his family while he'd waited at the Galax garage for yet another repair to his old van. He was supposed to catch up with the Clear Creek Boys in Richmond. He was eager to get back on the road. But this storm just might force a change of plans, at least for the night.

A figure hurried up the steps of the post office, shoulders hunched against the blowing snow. His coat flapped around his legs. He clutched a sheaf of papers in one hand while the other clamped his hat to his head.

Abby's father pulled the door open for him. "Heck of a storm, isn't it?"

"Not fit for man nor beast," the old man said. He took his wool hat from his head and beat the snow off against his leg. "But it's for a beast that I'm out in this weather."

"How's that?" Ian Whistler asked.

"Missing dog," Doc Pritchett said, holding up the flyers. "A good friend of mine's dog went missing a few weeks ago."

"That's sad," Abby's father said. "My little girl lost her dog back about five months ago. She's still tore up about it."

The old vet turned his back and surveyed the

223

community bulletin board. Notices for garage sales, pot-luck dinners, and moving sales covered the board.

"People get mighty attached to their pets," he said. He rearranged a few of the older notices. "My friend who lost this dog is recovering from a heart attack. I'm hoping if I put up some of these flyers for her, she'll stop worrying so much. But I have my doubts."

Doc Pritchett pinned a flyer to the middle of the bulletin board. He heard a gasp from behind him.

"A *sheltie*?" Abby's father said. "You're looking for a sheltie?"

"Why, yes, that's what he is. You're familiar with shelties?"

Ian nodded. "Yes, sir. That's the kind of dog my little girl lost too. Back in the fall."

"That's a shame. And a surprise too. They're normally loyal little dogs."

Abby's father rubbed the back of his neck. "My wife and daughter were in an accident up on the Blue Ridge Parkway in Virginia. The dog was in the back of the truck in a crate and was thrown out. We never found him."

"Did you put flyers up?"

"We did. Even had a photo of him and offered a reward. But it's been months and no word."

Doc Pritchett glanced back at the flyers. "A photograph would certainly help. Unfortunately, my friend hadn't had him that long, only a couple of months."

"So he's a puppy?"

The vet put his hat back on and rewound his scarf. "No, an adult. She found him half dead on her property. No collar or anything. She nursed him back to health. He ran off when she had her heart attack. Haven't seen him since."

Something nagged at the edge of Ian Whistler's mind. He was just about to ask what the sheltie looked like when the vet pushed open the door. "Well, I better get the rest of these put out. Don't want to be out on the roads any later than I have to." A gust of wind blew snow across the floor. "You take care now."

"You too, sir. And good luck finding your friend's dog." He watched the older man hurry to his car, then turned back to the flyer. Goose bumps ran up his arms as he read:

MISSING:
**MALE SHETLAND SHEEPDOG ABOUT
THREE YEARS OLD. MOSTLY RED IN
COLOR WITH WHITE PAWS, CHEST, AND
NECK. REWARD OFFERED. IF FOUND
PLEASE CALL IVY CALHOUN AT
276-555-2512**

Abby's father shook his head. Galax had to be more than two hundred miles from where the accident had happened. No dog could survive a journey that far, especially in the winter. Still . . . he read the description again. He didn't know much about shelties, but he did know Tam's red coat was unusual.

He removed the pin from the bulletin board and took one of the flyers. He folded it and stuffed it in his coat pocket.

Blowing snow ticked against the glass doors of the post office. It was snowing harder now. Abby's father sighed as he climbed into his old van. Looked like he'd be spending the night in Galax.

He leaned closer to the windshield and scrubbed his sleeve across the frosted window. "Not fit for man nor beast," he said aloud.

CHAPTER 33

Abby

"What's that you're doing?" Cheyenne asked from across our table in the cafeteria.

Without looking up from my sketch pad, I said, "I'm drawing a map."

She leaned across the table to get a better look. "Of what?"

"My daddy's music tour," I said.

Cheyenne returned to her book. "And how long's he been gone, as of today?"

I sighed. "Two weeks, three days, and four hours."

She shook her head and closed her book. Next to Olivia, she's the readingest person I know. "Better get used to it, girlfriend. Sometimes my daddy's gone for months at a time."

I wasn't at all sure I wanted Daddy to be a millionaire country singer.

"Harley's way into maps too," Cheyenne said. "He draws them on his computer, though."

I looked up. "No fooling?" I'd never met anybody but me who liked to draw maps.

"No fooling," she said. "He wants to be a cartographer when he grows up."

That didn't make much sense to me. "He wants to take pictures of cars?"

Cheyenne snorted. "No, you hillbilly. A cartographer is a professional mapmaker. Harley has all these expensive mapmaking programs on his computer. You can tell him to start at point A, give him points B and C and D, and tell him where you want to end up, and he can make a map of it. He can even tell you how long it will take you to get there . . . all kinds of stuff."

She plucked the sketch pad from my side of the table and studied my map. "Huh," she said, cocking her head to one side. "This is pretty cool. It's more like a story than an actual map, isn't it?"

"Yep," I said. I pointed to a snowy scene in Virginia that showed Daddy squinting through the windshield of his van. "That's Galax, where Daddy had to get the van fixed and ran into an unexpected snowstorm. And there," I said, pointing to a picture of Daddy sitting in a cornfield beside the road, playing his guitar, "is where the van broke down outside of Lexington, Kentucky, and Daddy had to wait forever for help. So he just decided to play his guitar while he waited."

"You don't have any pictures of him performing," she pointed out.

I closed up my pad. "No," I said. "We don't talk a whole lot about that when he calls. He's been playing in some big cities, though. Richmond, Virginia; Columbus, Ohio; Branson, Missouri. I think he's on his way to Kansas City now. . . ." I trailed off. "He sounds like he's having the time of his life, but I get tired just thinking about all those places.

"I know it makes Mama tired. She's been sleeping a lot since he's been gone." I twisted the end of my braid. "It's made her sick too. She doesn't know it, but I've heard her throwing up sometimes in the morning in the bathroom."

Cheyenne raised that one eyebrow of hers. I'd practiced like crazy trying to do that. My eyebrows, though, wanted to do everything together.

"But you know what?" I asked.

Cheyenne shook her head. "What?"

"We were driving to the Swishy Washy yesterday and we heard Daddy and his band on the radio!"

"I bet that made your mother feel better, didn't it?"

I frowned, remembering how Mama went from shocked

to happy to sad in five seconds flat. "Not really," I said. "I think it made her feel worse."

The bell rang. "I guess she's just heartsick without Daddy and the llamas," I said.

Cheyenne slung her book bag on her shoulder. "She's got you, though."

I shrugged. Mama had said me and her and Daddy were a three-legged dog without Meemaw. But without Daddy, we were like a two-legged dog. And I couldn't for the life of me see how a two-legged dog could get along.

That night, a bad dream about Tam woke me up. In it Tam was trapped in a cage of ice, with snow piling up all around him. He tried so hard to get out, but he couldn't, and there was nothing I could do to help him. I woke up, my heart pounding.

I got up to get a drink of water from the kitchen. The light was on. "Mama?" I called.

No answer.

I looked in her and Daddy's bedroom. She wasn't there.

Something told me to look out on the porch. And there she was, sitting in one of the chairs, her legs pulled up under her robe, looking at the full moon.

"Hey, Mama," I said.

"Hey, honey," she said. "What are you doing up this late?"

"I had a bad dream," I said. "About Tam."

Mama must've heard the tears all tied up in my throat. She held out her arms to me. "Come here, Abby."

I crawled into her lap, just like when I was a little-bitty thing. Problem was, I'd gotten bigger and Mama hadn't. But neither of us cared. She wrapped her arms around me and rested her chin on my head.

"Isn't it a beautiful moon?" she said with a sigh.

And it was. It was full and yellow as a gold coin. "Meemaw said Grandpa Bill called that a Carolina moon."

"Mmm . . . ," Mama murmured. "That's a beautiful name. It sounds like something he would've said."

She sighed. "I wish your dad were here to see it with us."

I sat up and looked at her. "But he is, Mama." And then I told her about his watching the same moon too.

"He just has to follow his north star, Mama," I said.

She smiled at me in a sad-but-happy way. "Is that right?"

"That's what he says. He says everybody has a north star, something that gives them a reason to keep going. Being a professional musician is his north star, just like Tam was—is—mine."

Mama and I gazed at that big ol' moon for a long while. I thought about all the times I'd watched the moon with Tam. Was he watching the moon too? I shivered in the night air.

"Let's get inside before you catch a cold," Mama said.

"It may be spring, but it's not that warm."

She tucked me under my quilt and kissed my forehead. "I love you, Abby Whistler," she said.

"I love you too, Mama."

Just as she was about to close my door, I sat up and said, "Mama, what's your north star?"

I knew what she'd say: her llamas. Or Daddy.

Instead, she smiled and said, "You are, Abby. You are."

CHAPTER 34

Tam

Scents and sounds Tam had not encountered in weeks rose to the top of the field in the early evening air: wood smoke, the slam of a car door, gasoline, the rich scent of turned earth. He smelled the horses standing in a barn, the apple trees on the verge of bloom.

He slipped back through the barbed-wire fence and into the forest. He trotted for another half mile on the road until the sound of water drew him away to a small stream. Ice edged the stream, thin as fine lace. A ledge of ice broke beneath his weight, plunging his front feet into the icy water. He drank long and deep until he could no longer feel his front paws. Tam was too tired and lonely to care.

He limped over to a lichen-covered outcropping and sniffed the damp moss. It smelled vaguely of skunk, but not too recent. Tam lay down with a sigh and licked the feeling back into his paws, then pulled sticks and leaves from his tail. His hip still hurt from his fight with the eagle.

Tam watched the moon rise above the far ridge, hanging full and golden between two peaks. All the night creatures stirred around him, beginning their ancient agreement between predator and prey. A fox barked in the hollow below the road.

Many times, Tam had watched the moon with his girl. Sometimes, they had watched from the front porch, with the sound of crickets and the big man's fiddle. Other times, they'd watched from the window seat in her bedroom. Tam had never known why the girl watched the moon with such longing. It had not mattered to him. He loved the moon because he loved the girl, the girl who held him close as she gazed into the night sky. He'd listened to her steady breathing, the *thump thump* of her heart. Her heartbeat had filled his world.

Tam could not know that his girl watched this same moon at this same moment, thinking of him. A dog can only know what he feels in his heart. Tam lifted his head, closed his eyes, and gave the long cry of a dog lost, cold, and lonely.

* * *

The next morning, Tam resumed his journey south on the Parkway. The road descended steeply, mile after mile, dropping away from the high, open spaces he had grown accustomed to. Every mile the road descended brought him closer to spring. And closer to the town of Blowing Rock.

By late afternoon, Tam watched children rush off the school bus from the cover of a forsythia hedge. He quivered in anticipation of seeing his girl, of hearing her voice cry, "Tam! Come here, Tam!" It was, after all, time. Time for his girl.

But, of course, she did not call.

Hunger drove Tam from beneath the hedge. He skirted the edges of the sprawling lawns of Green Briar Estates. He stayed always just out of sight, beyond the street lamps' widening skirts of light. Each house carried the sound of voices and the smell of food.

The largest of the houses sat at the end of the maze of streets, high up on a hill, surrounded by large oak trees.

Tam trotted up through the trees and watched the house. A cold wind blew through his thin frame. He shivered. But with the wind came the scent of fresh food. Tam searched the wind with his nose for the source of that smell. Then he found it. A large garbage can, the lid halfway off, crouched to the side of the house. Tam licked his lips and slipped from the trees.

After Tam had feasted from the overturned garbage can, he found a toolshed to bed down in. He listened as a late-March storm worried and tossed the tops of the trees. Somewhere, a hound bayed, and the delicate hooves of deer stirred the undergrowth. Tam dreamed of home.

For two more days, Tam raided the garbage can of Lilith McAllister and slept in her late husband's toolshed. For the first time in weeks, Tam began to feel rested and strong.

But on the third morning, as Tam stood on his hind legs just about to pull the can over, a voice cried, "Shoo! Get out of here, you bad dog, you!"

Tam froze. Guilt flooded his little body. How often had he heard the old woman in his home with the girl call him that same name, "bad dog," when he had gotten into the garbage?

He cowered and turned shame-filled eyes to the woman standing in the morning shadows. She flapped her hands at him. "You heard me, *shoo*! Get out of my garbage!"

Lilith McAllister watched, hands on her hips, as the dog scurried away into the woods. "Lord knows who *that* creature belongs to, but it doesn't belong in my garbage," she said to no one in particular.

After breakfast, she called Animal Control. By afternoon, the white truck pulled up in her driveway. "It's been getting in my garbage every blessed day," she said, showing the officer where she'd seen Tam early that morning.

"Did you notice if it had a collar or anything like that?" the man asked.

"I did not." Mrs. McAllister sniffed. "It looked like it had the mange of something, though," she said. "It looked wild."

The man whistled and called, "Here, doggy, doggy."

Tam cocked his head from his lookout at the edge of the woods.

The man walked around the property looking for signs of the dog. He pushed open the sagging door of the toolshed and shone his flashlight around.

"Looks like something's been sleeping in here," he called down to Mrs. McAllister. "Could be the dog."

The woman wrapped her arms around herself. "Good Lord, I can't have some wild dog eating out of my garbage cans and sleeping in my toolshed. Who knows what it'll do? You have to get rid of it."

The man in the uniform sighed. "Probably just a scared, hungry stray. Lots of them right now, what with so many folks losing their homes. Folks dump their pets out here in the wealthier areas, hoping someone will take them in. Our shelter's full of them."

"I want it gone," Mrs. McAllister cut him off.

"Yes, ma'am," the officer said. He went to his truck and returned a few minutes later with a cage.

"I'm going to bait this trap and set it up in the tool-shed. I reckon if the poor thing's hungry enough, we'll catch it pretty quick."

Tam watched warily as the man carried the cage up to the toolshed. His wariness changed to interest as the smell of meat drifted to him from inside the shed.

The officer stepped back into the sunlight. He scanned the woods for any sign of the dog. He headed back down the hill. "I'm willing to bet we catch it tonight."

"Won't be soon enough for me," Mrs. McAllister said.

"I'll check back first thing in the morning and see if we got our dog," the officer said.

Tam stayed away from the house and the shed until night-fall. He managed to knock over a few more trash cans, but the pickings were slim. At one house, an old hound dog chased him from the yard. At another house, two boys threw rocks at him. By the time Tam made his way back to the toolshed, he was hungry and bleeding.

Miraculously, the rich scent of meat greeted him inside the shed. Tam's heavy heart lifted. He pushed his way inside the odd metal box that held the meat. He grabbed the meat and *clank*! The door of the box slammed shut. Tam's heart filled with panic. He clawed and bit at the

238

metal bars. He threw his weight to one side and then the other. It was no use. He was trapped.

Sunlight slapped Tam in the face. He squinted at the open door of the shed.

"I heard all this barking and howling last night. It was quite a racket," a woman's voice said.

"He's probably in there, then." Tam recognized the man's voice from the day before.

Footsteps approached the trap. Tam pushed himself as far back into the tiny cage as he could. He needed to hide, he knew that. But he was trapped and there was nowhere to go.

A light from the man's hand shone in Tam's face. Tam turned his head away.

"Hey there, little guy," the man said. He ran the light from the flashlight across Tam's body. Tam shivered.

"Yeah, you look like you seen better days, that's for sure."

He grabbed the handle on the top of the trap and yanked Tam and the cage into the air. Tam scrambled in the wire cage, his eyes wide with fright.

The man carried the trap down the hill. He held it aloft for the woman to see. "Caught 'im," he said, grinning. "Just like I said."

Mrs. McAllister pulled her wool cardigan closer around

her shoulders and frowned at the trap. "And not a moment too soon," she said. "It could be rabid or something."

The officer shook his head. "Well, it's not your worry now," he said.

The officer put Tam and the trap into the back of his truck. He gazed at the dog, taking in Tam's dull, matted coat and skinny frame. He noted the dirty plaid collar around the dog's neck.

"I reckon you was someone's dog once," the man said to Tam.

Twenty minutes later, they pulled up in front of a squat, concrete building. The sound of frantic barking filled Tam with fear.

The man slung Tam and the trap onto a metal table inside the building. Tam cowered at the smell of fear and sadness and sickness.

"What you got there, Woodrow?"

"Another garbage dog out in Green Briar," the man said.

A large woman peered down at Tam. "Looks pretty bad off," she said, not unkindly. "Have you tried to handle him yet?"

The man shook his head. "Didn't want to get bit."

She laughed. "You're in the wrong line of work, Woodrow T. Farnsworth."

She flipped open the end of the cage and stuck her

fingers in and wiggled them. "Come here, little fella," she said in a high voice. "I won't hurt you."

Tam didn't budge.

She grabbed a dog biscuit from a jar and held it out to Tam. "Come here, little doggy. I've got a treat for a good boy."

Tam caught the words *treat* and *good boy*. He licked his lips and inched his way forward. But just as he stretched his neck out to take the treat, the woman grabbed him by his ruff and hauled him out of the trap.

She ran a large hand across his trembling frame. "Lord almighty," she said with a sigh. "He's a skinny one."

She felt around his neck. "Well, he does have a collar on, but no tags."

"Yep. Looks like he got into a fight or something too," the man said, pointing at the scabs on Tam's hip.

The woman scooped him up and carried him to an empty kennel. "No telling what he's been through." She deposited Tam onto the cold, concrete floor and clanked the wire door shut. "I'll give him some water and food after I get all the other kennels clean."

"You reckon there's any point in checking him for a microchip?" the officer asked.

They both watched as Tam investigated the dirty blanket in the back corner.

"Probably not," she said. "But I will, when I have a free minute."

All morning, Tam tried his best to shut out the sound of the other dogs' voices. One dog cried over and over, "Come get me! Come get me!" Another whimpered in her dreams of angry fists and being chased. Still another howled, "Where-oh-where have they gone?" Tam buried his head beneath the blanket and trembled.

"Oh, look how cute!" Tam awoke to the sound of a girl's voice. His heart leaped in his chest. He untangled himself from the blanket and stood.

"Is this one of the new ones?" the girl called over her shoulder.

The big woman came and stood beside the girl. "Yeah, got him in this morning. Haven't had time to fool with him yet, though. Been too busy."

"Can I go in and see him?" the girl asked. Tam wagged just the white tip of his tail.

The woman frowned. "I don't want you going in there by yourself. I need to check him for a chip, though. Let's both go in and check him over. Wait here while I get the scanner."

The girl knelt down in front of Tam's cage as the woman disappeared down the row of kennels. The girl pushed her fingers through the chain-link door and called softly to him. "Come here, little boy. I won't hurt you, I promise."

Tam took two hesitant steps toward her. He knew by now that this was not his girl. This girl calling him did not smell of apples and a swift creek. But still, the girl's voice was sweet. He walked over and sniffed the tips of her fingers. They smelled of peanut butter and milk. He licked first one finger, then the other.

The girl laughed. Tam wagged his tail.

"Looks like you've made friends."

Tam jumped at the sound of the big woman's voice.

"Let's go in and see if he's got a chip," the woman said to the girl.

They both knelt beside Tam. The girl encircled his chest with her arm and scratched him behind his ears. "That's a good boy," she cooed. "This won't hurt you."

The big woman held the scanner just above Tam's shoulders and clicked it on.

She scanned his right shoulder and between his shoulder blades. "Nothing," she grumbled. "Bloody waste of time."

Then she passed the scanner across his left shoulder. A light on the top of the wand blinked. She frowned. "It must be wrong."

She held the head of the scanner closer to Tam's skin and ran it slowly across his left shoulder.

"Well, I'll be dipped," she breathed.

"What is it?" the girl asked.

"He's got a chip! It's PAL and the number is"—she squinted at the tiny screen—"seven-one-six-five-seven."

The girl hugged Tam. "What do we do now?"

"We call the company and find out who that number is registered to," the woman said. "Then we pray that whoever cared enough to chip this dog is still there." The woman glanced at her watch. "We've got just enough time for a quick call."

The girl trotted behind the woman down the row of barking, howling dogs to a small, cluttered office. The woman paged through a notebook until she found the number she needed.

"First, let's call the company," she said to the girl. After the fourth ring, someone answered.

"Yes, ma'am, this is Dorothy Pollard at Watauga County Animal Shelter in Blowing Rock, North Carolina. I got a stray here we just picked up with one of your chips." Dorothy winked at the girl. The girl crossed her fingers.

"Okay, the number is seven-one-six-five-seven." Dorothy tapped a pencil on the edge of the desk. She put her hand over the mouthpiece. "She's checking the number in their database.

"Yes, I have something to write with," Dorothy said, sitting up straighter.

"Abby Whistler at Box Twenty-nine, Wild Cat Cove Road, Harmony Gap, North Carolina," Dorothy repeated as she wrote furiously on the pad of paper. "Is there a phone number?"

Dorothy glanced at the girl. The girl held up crossed fingers.

"Oh good." Dorothy nodded as she wrote down the phone number on her pad. "Thanks so much for your help."

Dorothy leaned back in her chair. "I can't believe it. Of all the dogs out there who have a microchip, that one's not the one I'd ever expect."

The girl clapped her hands. "Did they say what his name is?"

The woman glanced back down at her paper. "Yes, actually, they did. His name's Tam."

The bell on the front door of the shelter jingled. A voice called, "Julie, time to go home."

"Shoot," the girl said. "It's my mom. It must be five thirty."

She waved to her mother standing out at the front desk. "Can we try to call his family before I leave?"

"Sure," Dorothy said. She punched in the numbers and waited. Julie crossed her fingers again.

Dorothy shook her head and hung up the phone. "Busy. We'll try again tomorrow."

"Don't worry," Dorothy said as she walked Julie to the front door. "At least we know someone's there. He's not going anywhere between now and tomorrow."

Dorothy watched the slight girl and her mother walk to their car. The girl turned and called, "Don't forget, he's got a name now! It's Tam!"

Dorothy waved. "I won't forget!"

The woman locked the front door and turned off the computer and lights. "Not one single adoption today," she said, sighing.

She walked down the row of kennels, double-checking to make sure all the doors to the outside runs were closed. She stopped in front of Tam's cage. "You are one lucky dog, Tam."

Tam threw his ears forward at the sound of his name.

"Hopefully by this time tomorrow, you'll be back with your family, Tam, and I'll have one less dog to worry over."

Tam watched the woman as she walked down the hall and turned off the lights. The word she had spoken echoed in his mind. It was not the name the old woman had called him, the name not quite his name. This was *his* name. The name his girl murmured in his ear, shouted with joy. The name that linked him with her, that marked him as her dog. *Tam*. The name to lead him home.

CHAPTER 35

Abby

To: omcbuttars@carolinanet.com
From: "Abby Whistler" <sheltiegirl@carolinanet.com>
Date: Thursday, March 24 9:02 pm
Subject: Hey

Hey Olivia,

Just a quick note to say I'm real excited your grandpa is going to let you have two of Ginseng's kittens! I guess that will kind of make us relatives, since Ginseng is my grandmother's cat. I know how much you always wanted a kitten. Two is way more fun than one.

I talked with Meemaw for a long time last night. I told her, just like you told me to, how worried I am about Mama being tired and sick all the time. She said that just did not sound right, so then she talked to Mama for a long time. Mama seemed to feel better after that and ate a whole big bowl of mint chocolate chip ice cream. And she doesn't even like mint chocolate chip ice cream! I ate my share too, just so Mama wouldn't feel lonely eating hers.

Maybe we'll get through the next three weeks until Daddy's home. He called last night too, from Erie, Pennsylvania. I need to add that to my map.

Your friend,

Abby

P.S. I've been dreaming about Tam again.

Two days later, Mama had a big grin on her face when she picked me up from school. "Can I go over to Cheyenne's?" I asked, leaning in the truck window.

She shook her head and pushed open the passenger door. "Not today, honey."

"But Mama . . ."

She patted the car seat. "No buts, young lady. Get your fanny in this seat." She laughed like she'd made the funniest joke in the world. I rolled my eyes and waved to Cheyenne to go on home.

"What's gotten into you?" I grumbled.

"A big surprise," she said, grinning like a cat that's swallowed a canary.

My heart danced in my chest. "Is Daddy home?"

Her face fell just the tiniest bit. "Well, no. But I have a surprise that's the next best thing."

I got very still. Could it be something about Tam? I had a sudden lightning flash in a crevice of my brain. Maybe someone had called.

"Is it . . ." I couldn't get the words out.

"Just wait and see," she said.

I think I held my breath for the whole teetotal time we drove across town. I'd never in my life seen so many car-repair shops and pawnshops. Finally Mama swung the truck into the parking lot of the Greyhound bus station. She cut off the engine, looked over at me, and smiled.

I frowned. "I don't get it," I said. What would a bus station have to do with Tam?

Mama practically jumped out of the truck. "Come on, Abby. There's someone waiting inside for you." She held out her hand to me.

Someone waiting inside? That meant it wasn't Tam. I dragged over to where Mama waited for me.

She slipped her arm around my shoulder. I trudged beside her to the front doors of the bus station. And then another lightning bolt hit my brain: What if someone found Tam and sent him home on a bus? I'd read about that happening to a lost dog once.

I broke free of Mama's arm and ran into the bus station.

And there, in the middle of the lobby, grinning ear to ear, stood Meemaw.

She held out her arms to me. "Come here, Abby honey!"

My heart fell like a ton of bricks. How could I have been so stupid?

Mama gave me a little shove from behind. I walked into Meemaw's arms and buried my face in her coat so she couldn't see my tears. She smelled like home.

"Goodness gracious," Meemaw said, craning her neck practically out the truck window. "Have you ever seen such tall buildings?"

To tell you the truth, Meemaw showing up at the bus station in Nashville was just about as miraculous as if Tam had shown up there. I'd never known Meemaw to leave Harmony Gap. But here she was, and she said she'd be here until Daddy got back.

I pointed to a real tall building with pointy sides on the top. "That one there is the AT&T Building, but my friend Cheyenne says it looks like Batman's head."

Meemaw laughed. "She's right too."

Meemaw's eyes—the same eyes as Daddy's—danced with curiosity. They weren't scared like I was when I first saw the city.

We passed the Harris Teeter grocery store. "We'll get

groceries tomorrow," Mama said. "What y'all want for supper tonight?"

I wanted some of Meemaw's scratch biscuits and chicken and dumplings. And maybe an apple pie and—

"Pizza," Meemaw declared. "With extra pepperoni and olives."

The three of us sat around the kitchen table that night, finishing off the last of the pizza. Even Mama ate two slices, in between asking Meemaw a million and one questions about each of the llamas.

"They're just fine, Holly. I promise," Meemaw said. "Between all the attention they're getting from me and Mr. Singer and Olivia, they're spoiled rotten as eggs."

Mama sighed and wiped at her eyes. "I sure do miss them," she said.

Meemaw caught us up on all the news back home. "The biggest thing," she said, "is old Mr. and Mrs. Sutter's family has moved into their place."

The old Sutter farm was in between our farm and Olivia and her grandpa's place.

"I remember Mrs. Sutter passed a few months ago," Mama said. "I wondered if any of their children would move back or sell it."

"Their son from California has moved there with his family. He says he's going to bring that old Christmas tree farm back to life."

"They have any kids?" I asked.

"Four!" Meemaw beamed. "They have a little baby girl named Jasmine, a four-year-old girl named Sunny, and a twin boy and girl named Forrest and River. They're your age, Abby."

Meemaw got all dreamy-looking. "Been a long time since the cove had a bunch of young'uns in it."

"They nice?" Mama asked.

"Real nice," Meemaw said. "Why, just the other night they had me and Olivia and Mr. Singer all up to their place for dinner. We had a real good time. Olivia and the twin girl, River, hit it off like gangbusters."

I frowned. "Olivia hasn't said anything to me about it."

That night, for the first time in a long time, Meemaw and I brushed each other's hair before we went to bed. She'd be sleeping with me.

I told her all about my friends at school, especially Cheyenne Rivers. "And you know what, Meemaw?" I said.

"What, darlin'?"

"At first, everybody at school was afraid of her and wouldn't even try to be her friend. But it turns out, she's just real shy."

"Is that a fact?" I could feel Meemaw smiling behind me as she brushed and brushed my hair.

"Uh-huh," I said. "But now that she's been playing with us at recess and not wearing all those black clothes, people aren't so afraid of her.

"I'm still her best friend, though," I added.

Meemaw patted my shoulder. "You're still Olivia's best friend too."

I twisted around and gave Meemaw a hug. "I'm so glad you're here, Meemaw."

She kissed the top of my head. "Me too, sugar. You have no idea how much I purely missed you."

CHAPTER 36

Tam

"Any luck today?" Julie always asked first thing when she arrived at the animal shelter in the afternoons after school.

And every day, Dorothy Pollard shook her head. "Just got the answering machine. Again."

It had been a week since they'd discovered Tam's microchip. Julie thought perhaps his family was on vacation. But Dorothy knew, with each passing day they were less likely to find them.

Dorothy sighed, took off her glasses, and rubbed her eyes. Three more dogs had come to the shelter that day. Three more dogs without homes.

"I'm going to walk Tam," Julie called as she grabbed a leash.

"Okay," Dorothy said. "But don't forget about the other dogs. They need your attention too."

Tam walked into the kennel from the outdoor run. The other dogs barked and howled over the music on the radio and hurled themselves against their wire doors. That meant only one thing: Someone was coming.

He heard the girl's high voice as she greeted each of the dogs. They pleaded for her attention. "Pick me! Pick me!" "I'm best! I'm best!" But Tam knew he was her favorite. The dogs grumbled and whined as she opened his kennel door and clipped on the leash. "Let's go, Tam," she said.

Tam trotted along beside the girl in the brisk spring air. He liked this girl well enough. Her hands were gentle and she always had a special treat for him in her pocket. But she wasn't *his* girl. They did not belong to each other.

He stopped and scented the air to the south. He was stronger now, after a week of food and rest. It was time. Time to go to his girl. He pulled hard against the leash.

"No, Tam," the girl said. "We have to go back. I have to walk the other dogs too."

Tam pulled again. He felt the collar slip toward his ears. If only—

The girl scooped him up in her arms. "Come on, you stubborn boy."

* * *

255

Days passed, and with each passing day the urge to continue his journey home consumed Tam. He no longer ate his food. He stood impatient as the girl brushed him. He refused to come into the kennel in the evening from his outside run.

"How long until I can adopt him?" Julie asked Dorothy for the millionth time.

"In two more days, the waiting period will be up, and not a minute too soon," she grumbled. "Whoever would have thought that little dog would turn out to be so much trouble? Bad enough I have such a time getting him to come in at night before I leave. And now, just today, I discovered he's been digging under the fence."

Tam stood next to the wire door, waiting. Waiting for the gentle hands of the girl who was not his girl, waiting for the special treat she always had in her pocket.

As Julie opened the door to Tam's run and clipped on the leash, someone on the radio announced, "And now we have a song from a new group out of Nashville, the Clear Creek Boys. Give a listen. This is a group to watch."

Tam was taking the piece of cheese from her fingers when he heard, *There's a place high in the mountains, a place that I call home. . . .*

Tam froze: He knew that voice; he knew that music. It was the big man, the one who lived with his girl. That music was nights on a wide-plank porch, the big man singing, his girl singing, and Tam always, always by her side. That music was where he belonged: home.

He looked up at Julie and whined.

Julie laughed. "He's just got spring fever, don't you, Tam? A walk will do him good."

Julie led Tam outside for his afternoon walk. She chattered away the whole time. "I think I've about got my mom and dad talked into adopting you," she said. "We'll have so much fun. . . ."

Tam paid little mind to the girl's words as they walked south down the dirt road, toward the mountains. Her words were no more than a fly buzzing around his ear or the chattering of a mockingbird. What Tam heard, clearer now than ever, was the music of home, and the call inside him that said, *It's time . . . it's time.*

The girl stopped. "Gosh, I didn't mean to walk this far. Dorothy's going to skin me alive." She tugged on Tam's leash. "Come on, Tam. We've got to go back."

The girl turned back toward the kennel.

Tam stood stock-still, his brown eyes fixed on the mountains beyond.

The girl tugged harder. "Come *on*, Tam! We have to go."

Tam caught the word *come*. He had always been an obedient dog. He took one step, then two, toward the girl.

The wind carried the frantic barking from the shelter, the smell of fear and sadness. A school bus filled with the high, happy voices of children rattled past and disappeared south down the road.

The girl gave one long, hard pull on the leash. "Come on!"

Tam dipped his head and popped free of his collar and leash. Without a backward glance, he raced down the road after the school bus, raced toward the mountain and the only way home.

By evening, Tam had slipped through the vast apple orchards of Moses Cone Memorial Park. Less than a mile to the south stretched the Blue Ridge Parkway.

A thin curtain of snow blew through the trees. Tam shivered and his stomach grumbled. He was utterly miserable. He watched with longing the warm lights glowing in the huge white house at the top of a small rise.

Flat Top Manor had once been the grandest mansion south of Richmond, with its twenty-three rooms and gleaming white Victorian columns and arches. A sweeping, wraparound porch looked out over rolling white pine and hemlock forests, then up to the soaring peak of Grandfather Mountain.

Angus McIven had been groundskeeper of Flat Top Manor for as long as anyone could remember.

Angus took a long draw on his pipe and squinted through the snow at the small figure watching him from the edge of the orchard.

A sweet, sharp scent touched Tam's nose. The smell brought an image of the big man who lived in the house with the girl. Tam lifted his head and peered through the falling snow at the large white house and a man standing on the porch. For a moment, Tam was confused. Could it be the big man? Could that be his white house and his front porch? Tam whined, and walked hesitantly toward the house.

"Fox," Angus said to the old dog sitting next to him. He leaned against the stone railing, watching intently. He sucked on his pipe and exhaled slowly. "Looks like it's had a tough winter, Blue." The old hound dog thumped his bony tail on the porch floor.

Tam caught the low, soft voice of the man on the porch. He knew now this was not his house, nor the big man who lived there. But still, Tam was hungry.

Suddenly Tam smelled a new scent on the man: fear.

"Something's not right with him, Blue," the old man said, reaching for his blackthorn walking stick. "Could be sick, or worse."

Angus charged down the steps of the porch, waving his stick in the air. "Get out of here!"

Tam stopped dead in his tracks. His hackles rose even as he cowered closer to the ground. Here was another man, yelling and waving a stick at him. A stick that could be thrown; a stick that could explode and kill.

The old dog pulled himself up off the porch and

limped slowly down the steps to see what all the fuss was about. Like his master, his eyes were filmed over with cataracts; unlike his master, his nose worked just fine. He caught the scent of an intruder. He didn't know why the dog was frightened. But he did know his master was distressed and it was his job to protect him. The old hound drew himself up to his full height, raised his once-proud tail, and barked.

Between the man with the stick and the yelling and the barking dog, Tam knew he was not welcome. He whirled and dashed into the orchard. He heard the old dog give chase, the man call him back. Tam knew the dog would not follow him.

A week after his encounter with Angus McIven and the old hound, Tam wound his way through the high, wild reaches of the Blue Ridge. The Parkway left the towns and parks and people behind. Tam traveled over wild country, deep into the Linville Gorge Wilderness.

Although it was mid-April, winter was reluctant to leave the high country. Here, there were no flowering trees or tender, new grass. Deer still pawed through thin snow in search of food; ice still edged the creeks and pools. Here, the Blue Ridge Parkway was snow-packed.

Despite the snow and ice, Tam was filled with the fever of spring and hope. The warm, soft days as he traveled in the lower mountains had reminded him of all the things he and the girl would be doing, now that winter was over. There were creeks to explore, forests to say hello to. And, most importantly, agility training to do. He and the girl would work the course, getting faster and faster. Once he returned home, he would shake off the weight of the long winter and fly. Everything would finally be as it should.

Later that night, Tam's feet twitched in sleep. He yipped with joy. He had never felt so strong. He soared across the course in his dreams, flying toward the girl and her wide-open arms.

Something woke Tam. He blinked against the cold night sky. For a moment he didn't understand why he was so cold, so stiff, so hungry.

Then he heard it: the voices of coyotes calling ridge to ridge. He crawled from beneath the stony outcropping, stretched, and listened. The voices came again, closer this time. He lifted his nose to catch a scent. Nothing.

He limped down to the pool at the base of a small waterfall and drank. A cold wind lifted his matted fur and brought him a scent. A scent somehow familiar and somehow not.

Tam's heart lifted. He scrambled up the bank and over the rocky outcropping. There, in moonlight, stood a tall male coyote. The amber eyes glowed.

Tam wagged his tail. He knew this was not his friend,

the coyote; still how wonderful it would be to have a traveling companion again! Someone to hunt with and keep warm with at night.

A low rumble crept up the coyote's throat. Black lips pulled back from white teeth. Yellow eyes narrowed and hardened. Behind him, in the shadows, glowed several more pairs of coyote eyes.

This was not at all what Tam had expected. He pinned his ears back, turned his head to one side, not looking at the coyote.

The pack leader took a step toward Tam and sniffed. This dog was not strong, had not eaten well in some time. The coyote had noted Tam's limp as he walked up the bank from the pool. He smelled recently healed wounds on the dog.

As a general rule, the coyote despised dogs. Where dogs went, people followed close behind. People with their traps and guns, and their murdering ways. In his five years, the coyote had even killed a dog or two.

But what puzzled the coyote about this dog was what he *didn't* smell on him: the stink of man. Instead, the dog smelled of rich earth, blood, wind, leaves, and high, wild places.

The coyote stalked over to Tam, stiff-legged. He drew himself up tall, towering over the dog, flashing his teeth. Three more coyotes stepped from the shadows, their yellow eyes filled with hate and contempt.

Tam cowered, tucking his tail between his legs.

The three coyotes pressed closer. A small male crouched, preparing to leap upon the intruder.

Their leader flashed his teeth impatiently at them. They pinned their ears in apology and glanced at one another, bewildered.

The coyote ran his nose along the cowering dog, reading him from tip to tail. He read the miles and miles on Tam's paws. He read the months of cold nights beneath the stars. He read loneliness and determination.

The coyote stepped back, sat, and studied the dog through narrowed eyes. He knew this was no ordinary dog.

The coyote stood and yawned. This dog was not a threat. It would not bring man; it would not stay in his pack's territory. Besides, dogs were weak, used to being taken care of. And this dog was alone. No animal survived a high mountain winter without a companion, pack, or herd.

He barked one short command to his pack. With barely a backward glance, the coyotes disappeared beyond the moonlight.

CHAPTER 37

Abby

"So where's your grandmother want to go this weekend?" Cheyenne asked as we finished our lunch.

Here was another great big, fat surprise: Meemaw was the goingest person I'd ever seen! She wanted to see *everything* there was to see. She wanted to eat Nashville up.

Cheyenne had appointed herself as tour guide. She and Mr. Richard drove us all over the city and beyond, seeing the sights: the Country Music Hall of Fame and Museum, the old Ryman Auditorium, the state capitol. She showed us all kinds of famous people's homes and even got us VIP tickets to the Grand Ole Opry last weekend. I was about wore out.

"We're staying home this weekend," I said. "Daddy's coming back!"

The bell rang for the next class. "You're lucky," Cheyenne said with a sigh. "My dad doesn't get home for another week."

"Well, anyway," Cheyenne said, "ask her if she wants to go see the botanical gardens tomorrow after school. Richard thinks she'll like seeing that."

If I didn't know better, I'd swear Mr. Richard was sweet on Meemaw.

Friday night, Daddy called.

"Hey, peanut!" he yelled into the phone.

"Hey, Daddy! Where are you? You're still coming home, aren't you?"

"You better believe it," he said, and laughed. "If I had my way, I'd sprout wings and fly there in two minutes. But one of the headlights went out in the van. I don't dare drive any farther tonight."

He must've heard my heart sink, because he said, "Don't worry, though. I'm only about five hours away. I'll leave first thing in the morning. Y'all look for me about lunchtime."

"I'll be real happy when you get home, Daddy," I said.

"Me too, sugar," Daddy said. "I am bone-weary of life on the road." And he purely sounded like it too.

* * *

Having Daddy home was like Christmas, Thanksgiving, and all our birthdays rolled into one. From the minute he pulled into the driveway, Mama couldn't tear her eyes off him.

Meemaw about laughed herself to death when she saw his short, slicked-back hair and baby face. "Lord, lord," she said, wiping her eyes. "I wouldn't have recognized my own son if you'd come up and stood right in my face."

We spent most of the day and the night pestering him with questions and hearing his stories of life on the road. I showed him the map I'd made of his entire trip. He shook his head and pulled on the end of his nose. "You got this perfect, Abby. It makes me tired just looking at it."

"Did lots of people buy your CD, Daddy?" I asked.

"Yes, sugar, they did. More than we ever imagined would." But the funny thing was, he didn't sound too happy when he said that.

That night, Meemaw and I lay side by side in the bed. I listened to Mama and Daddy's voices drifting high and low from their bedroom. I heard Mama say something soft and tender, then Daddy practically yell, "You're *what*?" Then he let out a big whoop. He sure didn't sound that happy when he'd talked about selling all those music CDs.

"Meemaw, why do you think Daddy wasn't all that

266

happy about selling lots of CDs?"

She was quiet for a long time. I figured she must have fallen asleep. I was just about to roll over when she said, "Sometimes the thing you think is the most important isn't that big a deal, once you have it."

"But Daddy always said he had to follow his north star, and that being a professional musician was that star."

Meemaw rolled on her side to face me. "We learn new things about ourselves all the time, honey, all the time."

After breakfast Sunday morning, after Daddy unloaded all his instruments and things from the van, Mama said, "Abby, help me clean this van out. It looks like a pig's been living in it."

I crawled up in the van and handed garbage out to Mama—receipts and lists and doodles and bags and bags from fast-food places. I found empty soda cans and a pair of old gloves under the front seats. And way back was a piece of bright yellow paper. I grabbed it and was about to hand it out to Mama when something caught my eye. In big block letters were the words *SHETLAND SHEEPDOG.*

A chill ran from my toes all the way up to my scalp. My hands shook as I uncrumpled the paper. I could barely breathe as I read: *MISSING: MALE SHETLAND SHEEPDOG.* Just like in my dreams, I saw Tam. I saw him waiting for someone on a cabin porch, saw him wandering through the mountains cold and hungry, felt him trying to find a way home.

My knees buckled. I sat down hard on my behind.

"Abby, what's wrong?" Mama asked.

I held the paper out to her. She read it out loud, then looked at me. "Let's go find your father," she said.

"Ian!" she yelled as she banged through the front door.

Daddy was on the phone as usual. He held up a finger. "Just one second, Holly."

Mama grabbed the phone out of his hand and said to whoever was on the other end, "I'm sorry, my husband will have to call you back," and hung up the phone.

She thrust the flyer in Daddy's face. "What is this, Ian?"

Meemaw came up behind me and read the flyer over my shoulder. "Good Lord above," she whispered.

A million questions flew around the room.

"Do you think there's any chance?"

"How long ago was it?"

"Could it really be—"

"Why didn't you—"

Daddy waved his arms in the air like he was trying to fight off a bunch of angry bees. "Holly, Galax is more than two hundred miles from where we lost him! I didn't think there was any chance it was Tam. And then the weather was so bad and I was already running behind and . . ."

Mama glared at him, hands on her hips.

He glanced at me sitting there in the middle of the floor, clutching the flyer to my chest. In a lower voice he said, "I didn't want to get Abby's hopes up. I mean, what are the chances it was him after all this time?"

"I understand that Ian, but—" And they were at it again. I wanted to shout at them to just stop, to just shut up, but I couldn't. My heart hammered so hard in my chest, my words were beaten down.

And then in the middle of all this, Mama and Daddy arguing, me sitting in the middle of the floor, a voice strong as the mountains said, "You must call. Now."

Everybody stopped and looked at Meemaw. She stood tall, that still, faraway look on her face.

"Mama?" Daddy said. "You all right?"

Meemaw blinked, looked at us all like we were a house full of strangers. She snatched the paper from my hands, handed it to Daddy, and said again, "Call. Now."

"But Mama—"

Without a word, Meemaw grabbed the phone off the table. She looked at me, took a deep breath, and dialed.

We all held our breath as we waited for this Ivy Calhoun to answer the phone and answer my prayers.

After what seemed like forever and a day, Meemaw stood up a little straighter and said, "Yes, is this Mrs. Ivy Calhoun?"

She looked over at me and nodded.

"Are you looking for a missing sheltie, Mrs. Calhoun?"

Meemaw sat down on the couch and closed her eyes as she listened. I sat down next to her.

She took a deep breath and held my hand in hers, tight. "Mrs. Calhoun, my name is Agnes Whistler. I live in Harmony Gap, North Carolina, with my family. And I have a story to tell you."

CHAPTER 38

Tam

Tam passed beneath the long shadow of Mount Mitchell. The tops of the Black Mountains cut like shark's teeth through the bank of white clouds resting on the mountains' shoulders.

It was late April. Tam had traveled more than three hundred and forty miles in six months. He'd almost drowned, been chased by a bear, loved by a coyote, shot, and brought back to life by a kind, old woman. He had fought an eagle for a rabbit, had survived the brutal cold and snows of a high country winter. He had done all of this without thought or hesitation, because he knew he must return to his home with the girl.

Yet Tam was no longer the sheltie Abby knew. Gone

was the lustrous coat she had brushed until it glowed like firelight. Gone was the strong, sturdy frame and the easy, proud gait. Bones showed through his dirty, matted coat, torn and dull from mud and briars and too many days without food. Months of living wild had made him keen as any fox.

He knew the best places to sleep out of a cold wind, how to listen for faint life beneath the snow and earth, life he would kill and eat. He had learned the hard way to avoid at all costs porcupines, skunks, and most humans. He was more wild than not. It was only his love for the girl and his dreams of home that marked him as someone's dog.

The sun warmed Tam's bad shoulder. He had stopped to rest on a rocky outcropping. Wind slipped fine as silk through the thin needles of the pines. Restless with spring and hunger, Tam watched the meadow. He lowered his head to his paws and sighed.

Just as he closed his eyes, he heard a whisper of movement in the grass below. He cocked one ear toward the sound; his nose trembled. Slowly, very slowly, Tam raised his head. There beneath him, just on the edge of a tangle of rhododendron, was a rabbit. It was not a large rabbit, but it was bigger than anything Tam had eaten in a long while. His mouth watered and his stomach clenched.

Inch by inch, Tam gathered his legs beneath him. The wind carried his scent away from his prey. Nothing else existed for Tam except the rabbit and the distance between them.

The rabbit lowered her head to nibble at the new green grass, her back to Tam. The sheltie shot from his rocky perch, his front paws pinning the rabbit's hind end.

But the rabbit was keen and quick from the long winter months. She twisted from beneath her captor's paws and bolted into the thicket.

Tam tore after the rabbit, through fetterbush and dog-hobble. The rabbit squeezed free of the brush and darted into a maze of rhododendron. Tam barely broke stride. It was just like the weave poles on the agility course, all a matter of speed and control. Tam wove his way as quick and easy as water in a stream.

Sun shone through an opening in the rhododendron. The rabbit, seconds ahead of Tam, raced for the opening, cut left, and disappeared from sight.

Tam burst into the sunlight. The smell of hot, sweet blood filled the air. Tam skidded to a stop. The rabbit, *his* rabbit, hung like a rag from the mouth of a large cat.

The bobcat flattened his ears and growled around his full mouth. Tam knew this was not like the cats he had lived with at home. This cat was taller than he was and clearly hated him. The cat fixed him with hard, dark eyes. Still, the rabbit *was* his.

Tam took one step forward and growled.

The bobcat stepped back. Lichen-covered rocks behind and on both sides enclosed him. The bobcat glanced up to the ledge five feet above. Without the weight of the rabbit, he could easily spring to the top, well out of the dog's reach. If he wanted to eat this rabbit, he would have to find another way around the dog.

The bobcat dropped the kill. He had eaten recently. He spat and growled at the dog, to make a final point, and prepared to spring for the ledge.

Tam had never been particularly good at understanding why cats do what they do. They were a mystery to him. So when the cat dropped the rabbit, then spat and growled, Tam lunged forward to grab it.

The bobcat whirled, lashed at the dog with his long claws.

Fire raced across Tam's face. He yelped and snapped at the cat.

A stronger slap from the bobcat sent Tam tumbling backward. He screamed in pain, his vision blurred red. He pulled himself up and shook his head. Blood spattered the rocks and leaves. He looked for the cat. It was gone. And so was the rabbit.

Tam whimpered, pawed at his face. Bright blood smeared his white paw. He had never felt pain like this.

For several days, Tam pressed south. The deep wounds in his face festered. His eye throbbed.

He no longer tried to find food. He sought shelter when his body would take him no farther; he drank when he could no longer bear the raging fever in his body. Only one thing drove Tam: the instinct to go home.

The first few days, he covered many miles. By the fifth day, he barely managed a painful walk. His head hung low and lifeless, but his course south remained true.

Tam climbed the rocky trails to the top of the Craggy Gardens heath balds. The sound of snowplows scraping the last of the winter slush from the Parkway drifted up from below. The Parkway would open soon for the season.

Tam stood on that rocky, treeless crest and looked south through his one good eye to the endless ocean of mountains falling away and away before him. He swayed on his feet. With a last bit of strength, he scratched out a shallow bed in the thicket of laurel and blueberry bushes cowering on the exposed, high peak. He could go no farther. He curled in on his fevered body and slept.

CHAPTER 39

Abby

I grabbed Cheyenne as soon as we got out for recess. "I got to talk to you," I said, holding her tight by the arm.

We went over by the trees, away from the kickball game. I licked my lips and swallowed hard. "You remember me telling you about my lost dog, Tam?"

She frowned. "Sure I do."

I launched into my story about finding the flyer in Daddy's van and calling Mrs. Ivy Calhoun in Galax. I told how she'd found this little dog washed up on the banks of the river by her house.

"She thought it was a hurt fox at first because of the red and white fur," I'd told Cheyenne. "And that was my first clue the sheltie she'd found was Tam. Not many shelties have coats as red as his. She said he even had a white patch on the top of his head shaped like a star."

I told her how Mrs. Ivy Calhoun had nursed him back to health, that she'd said he was the smartest dog and best friend she'd ever had. "That's when I knew without a doubt the dog had to be Tam.

"She got real attached to him," I whispered, blinking back tears.

"Then how come he ran away?"

I explained about her heart attack and her son finding her there on the floor and chasing Tam away. "Tam must've been so scared," I sobbed.

"She was in the hospital for more than a week. She's been trying to find him ever since. She was just sick about the whole thing," I explained.

"And that was in February?" Cheyenne said.

"February twentieth, to be exact."

Cheyenne tried to blow out a whistle. Cheyenne can't whistle to save her life. "Where do you think he is, Abby?"

Looking north, I said, "On his way home."

This had been another big source of argument with Mama and Daddy: where had Tam gone and what the chances were of finding him *again* after two months.

Daddy had said he thought he was following the Blue Ridge Parkway south. Mama had said it was just a coincidence that Galax was close to the Parkway, and that didn't mean he was following it.

"That's still more than two hundred miles from the

Asheville area," Mama said. "He could be anywhere, if he's even still alive."

"You thought he was dead *before*," I said. "And now look."

Mama had touched my cheek. "I know, Abby, but that was months ago. I just don't want you to get all hopeful and then get your heart broken again."

"But I've *never* given up hope, Mama! I know he's on his way home."

Once again, Meemaw stepped in and calmed the storm. "The child's right, Holly," she said. "Tam's on his way home."

Pulling me to her and drawing herself up, Mama said, "With all due respect, Agnes, don't say that unless you really know it."

"I know it as sure as I know my own name," Meemaw said.

Cheyenne nodded in the bright spring sun. "Your grandmother's right. He's on his way back to you, just like in *Lassie Come-Home* and *The Incredible Journey*."

I paced back and forth. I was wound up tight as one of Daddy's fiddle strings. "But where would he be now?" I muttered. "Like Mama said, it's been months since Mrs. Calhoun lost him."

Miss Bettis blew her shiny silver whistle, signaling the

end of recess. I did not want to go back in that putrid school. I wanted to sprout wings and fly all the way to Virginia and look for Tam.

"Abby Whistler," Cheyenne said, hands on her hips, frowning down at me, "you of all people know."

"Know what?" I asked.

"Look at a map," she said.

"I did," I said. "But there's an awful lot of terra incognita between Galax, Virginia, and Harmony Gap."

She smiled. "Yeah but, you've got a secret weapon."

"Like what?"

"The Sight, Abby."

"I'm not sure I have the Sight like Meemaw," I said, and sighed.

The bell rang for the next class. Cheyenne shook her head. "You've got to trust yourself, Abby."

Two nights later, I got a great big clue from none other than Olivia McButtars.

"Abby," she said when I answered the phone, "I have some very important news. It's about Tam." I'd emailed Olivia right away after we'd talked with Mrs. Ivy Calhoun.

I could barely get words out past my heart jumping all around my throat. "What is it?"

"I checked the messages on your answering machine at your grandmother's house like she'd asked and—"

"Great bucket of gravy, Olivia," I said. "What *is* it?"

I heard her take a deep breath. "There were several messages from a shelter in Blowing Rock, North Carolina. They have Tam."

I almost fainted right onto the kitchen floor. "They have Tam?" I sobbed.

Mama and Daddy came in the kitchen. "What is it?" Mama mouthed.

I looked at her, grinning through my tears. "A shelter in North Carolina has Tam!"

Daddy's jaw dropped down to his knees. Mama grabbed a scrap of paper and a pencil and handed them to me.

I wrote down the number. "I'll call you back when I find out about Tam," I said to Olivia.

"I'm sorry I didn't check the answering machine sooner, Abby. Maybe if I'd . . ." Her little voice trailed off.

I wanted so bad right then to reach through that phone line and hug her. "Olivia Marie McButtars, you're the best friend ever."

"Thanks, Abby. So are you."

"I'll call you back as soon as I find out about Tam."

Mama dialed the number of the shelter for me. My hands shook so bad, I couldn't do it. She handed me the phone.

It rang once, twice—

Please answer, please answer, I prayed.

Finally, on the fourth ring, a woman's voice said, "Hello, Watauga County Animal Shelter."

"Yes, ma'am," I said, holding the phone tight. "My name is Abby Whistler and I believe you have my dog, Tam."

Mama and Daddy grinned at each other.

Every bit of my brain filled with a movie of us driving up there, me running into the shelter, throwing open his cage door, and—

"I'm sorry, honey," the woman said. "He's not here anymore."

"He *what*?" Cheyenne said, when I told her the latest chapter of Tam's story the next day at lunch.

I buried my head in my arms. "I can't believe it either. But yes, he ran away two putrid, putrid weeks ago."

Cheyenne tapped her fork against her cheek. "But that's south of Virginia, right?"

I looked up from my arms. "Yeah, in North Carolina."

"Anywhere near the Blue Ridge Parkway?"

I sat up straighter. "Yeah, actually. Real near." I knew this from looking at Daddy's road atlas the night before.

Cheyenne nodded. "You come home with me after school tomorrow. It's time to put Harley to work."

"Really?" I asked. "You think he'd help me?"

Cheyenne cocked her head to one side, the sun shining

on her black hair. "Why wouldn't he? He loves a challenging map project. Besides, you're my best friend."

I looked at her then and thought about her and Olivia and that Mrs. Ivy Calhoun—all the people helping me and Tam along the way. I'd always thought I liked animals more than people. But if I could have talked to Tam right then, I'd have told him I'd learned that humans can make fine friends too. And Tam would've understood, because Tam always understood.

CHAPTER 40

Tam

For three days, a cold, steady drizzle washed the tops of Craggy Gardens. Banks of thick fog came and went between thin rain. The fog and the rain wove its way in and out of Tam's dreams. From time to time, thirst drove him from beneath his shelter of shrubs. He limped to the small pool of rainwater cupped in a depression of granite. He drank just enough to cool the fever in his body, then returned to his bed and dreamed.

On the fourth day, a sound woke the dog. Tam lifted his head and peered into the fog. The pain in his face made him whimper. Still, he stared. There was something—a familiar form—just on the edge of the fog. With great effort, Tam crawled from beneath the bushes and searched for a scent. It was a scent he knew, a scent like a dog but not quite. A scent laced with companionship and safety. It was the scent of his friend, the little coyote.

Tam wagged his dirty, matted tail and whimpered a greeting. His heart filled with joy.

The coyote wagged her beautiful, full tail, her amber eyes shining. She drifted closer, beckoning Tam to follow, then melted into the mist.

Tam followed her across the craggy heath, the coyote always just in sight. When he faltered or stopped, she appeared out of the mist, silent and insubstantial. Tam would rise with a groan and follow. To be with her, and the safety and warmth of her body, would be enough.

In this way, she led him down the mountain. By nightfall, Tam reached the picnic area behind the Craggy Gardens Visitor Center, exhausted. He made a bed inside the protection of a tall tangle of rhododendron, the overarching branches forming a perfect tunnel. The spirit of the little coyote slipped back into his dreams.

The man and his daughter took the Blue Ridge Parkway up to Craggy Gardens every spring as soon as the roads opened. Some years, the laurel and rhododendron blanketed the mountain with a candy-colored display of pink, white, and red. Other years, the man and his daughter waded through snow. In late summer, he and his daughter and wife filled plastic milk jugs full of blueberries. This year, snow crusted the sides of the recently plowed road. Drifts of snow still pooled in the shaded parts of the forests.

"Don't know how good a hike it's going to be today, Emma," her father said, straining to see through the fog from the car window.

"Doesn't look like spring made it yet," the girl said.

They drove slowly up the Parkway in comfortable silence. At last, they pulled into the parking lot of the Craggy Gardens Visitor Center. "Let's go in and see if they have any of that free hot chocolate," her father said.

"How long's the road been open?" Emma's father asked the ranger behind the counter.

"Not long," she said. "It was a tough winter up here, and one of the worst Aprils I've ever seen. Didn't think the snow would ever stop. I heard up around Mount Mitchell they may not open the road for a couple more weeks."

The ranger handed two Styrofoam cups of steaming hot chocolate across the counter.

The man blew across his cup to cool his first sip. "How far up can we drive?"

"It's plowed to Glassmine Falls Overlook, but I wouldn't advise going up there. Judging by what we've had the last three days down here, the road up is probably a sheet of ice."

Emma's father rested his hand on her shoulder. "Sorry, bug. Guess this is going to be a shorter trip this year. But we can at least have a little picnic before we head back."

Emma and her father ate their ham sandwiches at a picnic table in a small clearing behind the Visitor Center. A crow watched from a limb above their table. A rabbit huddled beneath a low bush, ears standing at attention, black nose twitching.

"Fog's thick as pea soup," her father commented.

"Mama's navy bean soup," Emma added.

The high, faraway voice of a girl awakened Tam. The voice floated through the fog accompanied by the low, deep voice of a man.

Tam lifted his head and listened. He could not see if the voice belonged to his girl. The thick fog kept the wind from carrying scent to him. But memories of gentle hands; high green grass; a special place by a creek; a warm, soft bed; and a bowl of food washed over him. Trembling with effort and hope, he pulled himself to his feet and followed the voices.

"Look, Dad," Emma said, pointing to the tunnel of rhododendron on the far side of the meadow.

The man squinted through the mist where his daughter pointed. A small creature slipped in and out of the shadows, coming toward them.

"What is it, Dad?" Emma asked.

He leaned forward. As the animal stepped from the tunnel into the weak light of the clearing, he saw a red coat, white chest, and the flick of a white-tipped tail.

The man touched his daughter's arm. "Kind of looks like a fox, doesn't it?"

The girl leaned forward, squinting. "Kind of. But Daddy, it looks so scrawny."

The animal staggered toward them.

Not taking his eyes off the animal, he said, "You're right. It looks like it's in bad shape."

Emma broke off a piece of ham from her sandwich. "Maybe I should give it some of my sandwich."

Tam whimpered and took another step forward.

The man frowned. "No, honey," he said. "It looks sick. It might be dangerous. I think we better leave."

"But Daddy—"

"Let's *go*, Emma. We'll tell the ranger about it on the way out. She should know about it, just in case."

Tam watched the girl leave. He whimpered and tried to follow. He had come so far to find her, and now she was leaving him. This was not at all how it should be. His faithful heart utterly broke.

"It's following us," the man said. "There's got to be something wrong with it." He grabbed his half-empty soda can and hurled it. "Get out of here!" he cried.

"Daddy, don't!"

The can glanced off the boulder with a sound like a gunshot. Tam froze. The man yelled again. Memories—of exploding glass, foul-smelling liquid, the roar of a rifle, the shouting man in the old woman's cabin—overwhelmed him. He whirled and ran back into the mist and shadows.

Ranger Lora Jean Graham looked up as the man pushed open the door of the visitors center. Jerking his thumb back over his shoulder, he said, "My daughter and I just saw a fox over by the picnic area."

The ranger smiled. "We see them from time to time. They won't bother you."

"This one seemed aggressive. And it looked sick. You better trap it or something. It's probably dangerous."

Lora Jean frowned. In all the years she'd worked up here, she'd never heard of a fox being aggressive. "We've never had a problem with a fox before. You may be right about it being sick or hurt. I'll call Fish and Wildlife as soon as I get a minute."

She watched out the front windows as the taillights of the man's car disappeared into the fog. She walked the short path behind the Visitor Center to the picnic area. The man and his daughter had left food on the table. She shook her head as she gathered up the garbage. No wonder a fox was coming around.

The sun broke through the mist. The gleam of the

soda can caught the crow's eye. He swooped down from the hemlock, pecked gleefully at the can.

"Geez, what's *that* doing over there?" Ranger Graham muttered.

As she bent to pick up the can, she saw small, canine prints in the wet earth. They looked fairly new. "Could be a fox," she said to the crow. "About the right size." Something wet and dark shown on the grass beside the prints. She touched her finger to the grass. Blood.

CHAPTER 41

Abby

"Whoa," Harley said, letting out a whistle. "I've never seen anything like this."

He and Cheyenne studied the Tam Map I'd made the night before. I'd gotten a long roll of butcher paper and mapped out the last six months, from the agility trial to now. I mapped out everything we'd done and seen and heard and felt. I mapped out all my fears and hopes—and even the dreams I'd had about Tam. All those things were tied up inside me like crisscrossing animal tracks in the snow. So I laid it all out on a map. It was the biggest map I'd ever drawn.

But I'd been practical too. I wrote in every date and exact place I knew of. I even put in what the weather had been like, if I knew. It had been hard to be that practical, but I did it for Tam.

"I feel like a bird, way up in the sky, looking down on every little thing that's happening," Cheyenne said.

Harley clapped his hands together. "Let's get to work," he said.

He tapped the top corner of the map. "Looks like you lost him on October twenty-fourth." He typed the date into his computer, then glanced at the date on a real fancy-looking watch. "And today is April thirtieth." He typed that into the computer too.

Cheyenne and I peered over his shoulder as he typed all this information into his fancy map program. He muttered stuff to himself like, "Gotta overlay the GPS," and "Calculate speed per elevation gain."

Finally, he sat back and clicked Print. In seconds, his printer spit out a real live map. In color.

"Here you go," he said, handing it to me.

I looked at it and shook my head. "What does it say?"

Harley sighed. He took the map back, smoothed it out on the desk. With a red pen, he circled an area at the end of the map. "There," he said, jabbing at the red circle. "If all my calculations are right, that's where your dog is."

"Craggy Gardens?" Daddy asked for the millionth time, rubbing the back of his neck.

I waved Harley's map in Mama and Daddy's faces again. "That's what Harley figured out, and he's a genius when it comes to maps. He's even going to be a professional mapmaker when he grows up."

Mama and Daddy exchanged one of those looks.

"And we used a map I made too. It's the best one I've ever made, and y'all are always saying how my maps are practically perfect."

"But Abby," Mama said, "the maps are just based on speculation. I agree it does appear he's following the Blue Ridge Parkway, but we don't *know*."

I wanted to scream, but instead I took a deep breath. "It's not just speculation, Mama. Harley had this fancy mapping program on his computer that probably cost a million dollars. Harley put in the exact coordinates of all the places we know Tam has been. It even calculated how fast Tam might be traveling. And it says Tam's at Craggy Gardens by now."

Mama sighed.

I turned to Daddy for help. "Daddy, can't we go up there and look? The Craggy Gardens ranger station is the only one in the area. I just know we'll find him. We could leave tomorrow and—"

"That's a long ways up there, sugar, and we've all got a busy week." He looked at Mama and smiled a goofy kind of smile. "Your mama and I have an important appointment tomorrow. Maybe by the weekend we can head up there," he said.

"That's too long to wait!" I cried. "He's trying to get home!"

"Abby," Mama said, "we can't just run off from school and our jobs on the slim chance a computer's right and Tam's up there."

"Mama, please," I begged.

She smoothed my hair back from my face. "I'll tell you what, let's look up the phone number of the Craggy Gardens ranger station on the internet and give them a call. We can let them know to look for him." She peered into my eyes. "Okay?"

"We can even email them a picture of Tam," Daddy said, like it was the best idea in the world.

But it wasn't. The only best idea in the world was for me to somehow get to Tam.

CHAPTER 42

❦

Tam

The next morning, Lora Jean Graham unlocked the Craggy Gardens Visitor Center just as the sun touched the tops of the far ridge. "Looks like it's going to be a nice day," she said to the crow sitting in the dogwood tree.

Lora Jean filled large pots for coffee and heated water for hot chocolate. Then she called Fish and Wildlife. She doubted the fox the man claimed he saw was dangerous. But it might be sick or hurt, and she had a particular fondness for foxes. Best to trap it and help it.

Within an hour, Percy Woods stomped into the Visitor Center, rubbing his hands together. "Turned off cold again," he grumbled. "This durned spring can't seem to make up its mind whether it's coming or going."

The ranger handed him a cup of steaming coffee.

"Thank you kindly, Lora Jean."

The ranger smiled. "No problem, Percy. You bring me a trap?"

Percy nodded. "Yes, ma'am. Got the trap and bait out in the truck."

Lora Jean pulled on her coat. "Finish up your coffee and let's get that trap situated."

Just as they were about to head out the door, the phone rang. The ranger sighed. A phone call this early could mean only one thing: her supervisor's latest Big Idea.

"Sit tight, Percy. I'll just be a minute."

But it was not her supervisor calling.

"No, ma'am," Lora Jean said, frowning. "I sure haven't seen a dog. The weather's still pretty bad up here and, of course, we've only been open a few days."

"A shelter up in Blowing Rock had him, you say?"

Lora Jean nodded her head as she listened. "With all due respect, ma'am, Blowing Rock is a long ways away and it's very rough terrain between there and here."

She grabbed a pencil and a piece of paper. "Yes, Mrs. Whistler, I have something to write with." The ranger scribbled a number down. "I'll watch out for him, ma'am," she said. "But I really don't think—"

She rolled her eyes at Percy. "Yes, I will. And I'll watch

for the email. Good-bye."

"Some folks in Nashville lost their dog back in the fall way up on the Virginia end of the Parkway. For some reason they think it may be in this area," Lora Jean said, heading over to the door.

Percy shook his head. In his opinion, people put too much stock in the intelligence of domesticated dogs. "Nobody's pet dog would make it this far during the winter we've had."

"That's what I tried to tell her," Lora Jean said. "But you know how city people are."

Lora Jean showed Percy where the man claimed to have seen the fox.

"You saw prints?" he asked.

"Yeah," she said, pointing to the dirt. "They looked to be about the right size. I also saw some blood and some red hair caught on the bush here."

Percy set and baited the trap.

He straightened up and eyed the crow sitting in the hemlock tree. "Well, you won't catch a healthy fox, but I reckon you'll catch something. I'll leave you extra bait."

Percy climbed in his truck. Sleet pattered against the windshield. "You call me if you *do* get a fox. I'll come right over. If you catch one, it'll be sickly. I don't want you messing with it."

Lora Jean Graham touched two fingers to her ranger's hat. "Yes, *sir*, Mr. Woods!"

*　*　*

Tam heard voices. He raised his head and listened, but the voices did not come closer. When they moved away, he laid his head across his paws and slept. The fever in his body wrapped him in such a deep sleep, he did not smell the fresh meat in the trap thirty feet away. He did not hear the angry cry of the raccoon when the door to the trap snapped shut.

The ranger wiped the last of the coffee drips off the counter and readied the Visitor Center for closing. She pulled on her coat and hat. "Guess I better check that trap," she said.

The raccoon spat and hissed at Lora Jean. "Sorry, little guy," she said. She pulled up on the piece of twine tied to the trap door. "Shoo! Go on home now," she said. She rebaited and set the trap. The crow chortled from the tree above. "And with my luck, I'll catch a possum next," the ranger said.

That night, the rhododendron tunnel came alive with the comings and goings of all manner of night creatures. Feet scurried and scuffled within inches of Tam's nose. He did not raise his head to snap at them. Fever and hopelessness dulled his rich brown eyes. Tam was beyond hunger. He was beyond thirst. He was beyond caring. His body and loyal heart that had carried him so far through so much were failing.

CHAPTER 43

Abby

I didn't even say hey to Cheyenne when I called her Sunday night. "I need a favor, Cheyenne. A big favor."

"What?"

"I need you to call my house after school tomorrow and tell Meemaw I'm going over to your house," I said.

Cheyenne laughed. "Well, duh. We've only done that a million times. That's no big deal."

I licked my lips. "And I need you to invite me to spend the night."

Cheyenne's voice frowned. "You think your mom's going to let you spend the night on a school night? She never has before."

I could just see her studying me through the phone

lines. "What are you up to, Abby Whistler?"

All in a great big rush, I said, "I got to get up to Craggy Gardens and find Tam *now*, Cheyenne. I had this terrible dream about him last night and he was trapped in this tunnel and he was almost dead and . . ." I couldn't choke out any more, remembering that awful dream.

"So what are you going to do?"

"I'm going up there myself. I'm leaving first thing in the morning."

"And?"

I twisted the phone cord around and around my finger. "And Mama and Daddy don't know. But they don't believe me when I tell them this weekend will be too late!"

"But—"

"I've never asked you for anything, Cheyenne. But could you please, please cover for me so I can get a head start?"

"How in the world are you going to get all the way up there? It's not like you can drive," she pointed out.

I licked my lips. "I'm going to hitchhike."

I could've sworn I heard her jaw drop.

"But Abby, that's at least a three- or four-hour drive," Cheyenne said in this exasperated voice. "And besides, who knows what kind of wacko might pick you up."

"You're not going to talk me out of this," I snapped.

"I've got to do this for Tam. Besides, you're the one who told me to trust myself."

Cheyenne laughed. "I wasn't going to say don't do it. I was just going to say, why hitchhike when you can take a limo?"

CHAPTER 44

〜〜⚭〜〜

Tam

Lora Jean Graham was right. The next morning when she checked the trap, a possum crouched in the corner. She sighed. "This is hopeless."

She let the possum loose and carried the trap back to the Visitor Center. She wasn't sure it was worth the trouble of baiting and setting it again. She had a feeling the fox was nowhere to be found. "Well," she said, "three's the charm. I'll bait it extra good this time."

She placed the trap just to the side of the opening of the rhododendron tunnel. She studied the variety of tracks leading in and out of the opening. She walked inside and looked up at the branches arching and embracing overhead.

She started to walk farther along the shaded path when she heard a car pull into the parking lot. Voices. She sighed, took one last look, and turned around. "Time to get back to work," she said.

The ranger glanced at the computer screen as she stationed herself behind the desk. A tiny envelope flashed, indicating she'd received a new email. "Wonder who that's from," she muttered as she clicked on the envelope. The image of a red and white dog with long fur, shining eyes, and a white star-shaped mark on its head shone from the screen. Below the photograph, the email read: *His name is Tam. He is microchipped. We appreciate your help. Holly Whistler*

"He's a pretty little dog, I'll say that," Lora Jean said as she gazed admiringly at the photograph of Tam. "Looks like one of those little collies."

The front door swung open. A harried-looking mother and father followed a pack of four screaming, laughing children into the visitor center. "We wanna see some deers! Now!" one of the children demanded.

Lora Jean sighed and clicked out of her email. It was going to be one of those days.

For the first time in days, the sun shone strong and warm on the mountain. Butterflies swarmed the laurel and rhododendron. Birds sang and fluffed their feathers in the sun. A fox sunned itself on a warm rock and groomed its tail.

And for the first time in days, the sun's afternoon light found Tam. It pulled him from a fevered sleep and stirred a longing, a message, in his soul.

It was time. He must watch for his girl.

With every bit of strength and hope he had, Tam pulled himself to his feet. He took two steps toward the sunlight at the opening of the tunnel. There. If he could just get there, he could find her and everything would finally be as it should be.

He took several more steps. Fever swam through his small body. It meant nothing to Tam.

And then it happened: His muscles refused to carry him. His back legs quivered, then sank beneath him. He commanded them to rise. They refused.

Tam whined in frustration.

It was time! He tried to rise but fell.

A human watching this poor dog pull itself along, foot by foot, would wonder at its motivation. A human would surmise it was purely the instinct to survive that drove this dog. A human could not guess at the measure of love that beat in the little dog's true heart.

At last, Tam could go no farther. He was tired, so tired.

Tam lay on his side, panting. He groaned under the weight of his disappointment. He took one last look at the sunlight beyond and closed his eyes. He could do no more.

CHAPTER 45

Abby

I twisted around in the backseat of the limo and watched the tall, shiny buildings of Nashville grow to the size of specks.

Cheyenne pulled the earbuds of her iPod out of her ears and said, "The cops aren't after us, Abby. Stop worrying."

"I ain't worried," I said. But I surely was. I worried I'd see Mama's truck or Daddy's van speeding up behind us, flashing lights and honking horns.

And I worried we wouldn't get to Tam in time.

I heard Mr. Richard mumble something from the front of the car about "fool idea" and "I reckon I'm the only one smart enough to be worried."

I couldn't believe Mr. Richard had agreed to drive us

up there in secret. When I'd asked Cheyenne why he was doing this, she said, "He's the one who gave me Dusty. He loves her almost as much as I do."

"So?" I'd said.

"So," she said, "you saved her life, remember? Besides, he believes in your grandmother's Sight."

I took the end of my braid out of my mouth. "Your parents are probably going to skin you alive," I said.

Cheyenne yawned and propped a foot on the back of the driver's seat. "That's all right. I've been a good girl for too long. I need to keep them on their toes," she said, winking.

We both stared out the windows as the long black car purred along the interstate, Harley's map between us.

"What about you, though?" she asked. "What do you think your folks will do when they find out you've run off?"

I rubbed Tam's collar between my fingers. "They got bigger fish to fry than me right now," I said, and sighed.

That one eyebrow of Cheyenne's arched up. "Like what?"

"Well, for starters, half of Daddy's band—Cue Ball and Jeb Stuart—left and went back to Harmony Gap. They said they'd had enough of Nashville ways and wanted to go back where they could be themselves." Poor Daddy. He was fit to be tied.

I lowered my voice and whispered, "But the biggest thing is"—I glanced at the back of Mr. Richard's head—"Mama's *pregnant*!" I still couldn't believe it.

Cheyenne grinned. "Well, that certainly explains a lot."

Before I could ask her what she meant, she asked, "What about your grandmother? Did she suspect you were going to look for Tam?"

I remembered Meemaw saying to me just before I fell asleep the night before, "Hurry, Abby."

I blinked back tears. "She knows me pretty well, I reckon."

The sky got darker the closer we got to the mountains. Mr. Richard turned on the heat. As we crossed into North Carolina, a big gust of wind about blew us off the road. Within seconds, sleet pelted the car.

"Look, Abby." Cheyenne pointed to a green and white sign.

"Asheville, twenty-five miles," I read out loud.

I leaned forward and said to Mr. Richard, "Just before we get to Asheville, we'll see signs for the Blue Ridge Parkway."

"And then how far is it to this place we're going after that?" Mr. Richard asked.

I studied the map on my lap. "Looks like about another ten miles or so."

"Lord, Lord," Mr. Richard said as the wipers slapped at the snow building up on the windshield.

I closed my eyes and prayed for the snow to stop, for the car to go faster, for Tam to hang on.

CHAPTER 46

∽)⊂∽

Tam

Tam did not stir.

He did not stir as the animals around him hunted and were hunted. He did not stir as the young ones played under the watchful eyes of the adults, and the old ones dreamed of full bellies and warm summer sun.

He did not stir as wind and snow and cold lashed Craggy Gardens, bending the tops of the trees low and blanketing the new, green grass.

Instead, Tam dreamed his way through long streams of memory. He dreamed of drinking warm milk alongside his sisters, faces pressed into his mother's side. He dreamed of hot meals beside the stove and a soft bed. He dreamed of hunting with a young coyote, the taste of hot blood and snap of bone. He dreamed of an old woman's soft voice and gentle hands.

But mostly he dreamed of his girl. He ran young and strong across meadows and through agility courses. He waited and watched. And when it was time, she came. He flew into her arms, covered her face with kisses. She cradled him in her arms and carried him over the mountains, across wide rivers, to a lush, green meadow, the *thump thump* of her heart filling his world.

CHAPTER 47

Abby

The three of us stared at the sign on the gate, dumbfounded.

"I can't believe it," Cheyenne cried for the third time. "How can the road be *closed*?" She poked her head out the car window. "I mean, give me a break! It's May third! It's just a little snow!"

Mr. Richard shook his head. "It's more than 'just a little snow,' Miss Cheyenne."

And it was true. The temperature must've dropped a zillion degrees. I'd guess there was already a good three inches of snow on the road, probably ice underneath.

I dropped my head in my hands and pressed hard against my eyeballs to keep from crying. It just wasn't fair.

Tam had come so far, and so had we.

I felt Cheyenne's hand on my back. "I'm sorry, Abby," she said, sniffling. "We'll go up as soon as the weather clears and they open the road."

But I wasn't listening to her. My brain was filling up with flashes, pictures of Tam. Tam swept away in a river, Tam cold and hungry and scared, Tam being shot at, Tam being chased by something big and black, Tam walking mile after mile after mile—all these pictures, clear as anything, flashing one after another. But always, Tam on his way home to me. And now it was time for me to bring him home.

I threw open the car door and bounded out into the snow. The wind about snatched me bald, but I didn't care.

"Time's a-wasting!" I called back to Cheyenne and Mr. Richard as I ducked under the gate across the road.

"But Abby!" Cheyenne hollered into the wind. "It's eight miles up to Craggy Gardens!"

"And Tam's come four hundred!" I yelled as I jogged up the road, slipping and sliding.

The snow stung my eyes and face. It seemed like, for every step I took, I slid two steps back. Over and over I prayed, *Please don't let me be too late.*

I had no idea how far I ran up the Parkway in the snow. I kept putting one foot in front of the other, even after my feet were so wet and cold, I couldn't feel them.

I'd just jogged around a hairpin turn. The snow was blowing in my face so hard, I could hardly see. Next thing I knew, I was flying up in the air, then hitting the asphalt hard. I stood up and looked back. A tree limb lay in the road. I hadn't even seen it.

My hands were skinned from hitting the ground. "Gotta keep going," I said through my chattering teeth.

I took one step forward and slid and skittered on a patch of ice. "No, no, no!" I cried into that putrid wind and snow. Every muscle in my body hurt. I heard Daddy's voice in my ear. *Never give up on your dream, Abby.* I heard Meemaw's voice say, *Hurry, Abby. Hurry.*

I grabbed a branch and used it like a walking stick to keep me steady on the ice. I picked my way up the road a little ways, and was going along pretty good, all things considered, until—

Snap! The stick broke and I toppled over into the snow. I tried to push myself up but slid back down to the ground again, landing hard on my wrist.

This time, I could not get up. "Please help me get to Tam," I prayed right out loud. "I've got to get to him."

And then, just like in a dream, I heard a sound. It was not the sound of wild wind screaming in the branches. It was not the sound of snow rattling the leaves.

Was it the sound of a car? I held my breath and listened as hard as my ears could hear.

No, not a car. A van.

I pushed myself upright and squinted into the storm. Daddy's old VW van crawled around that hairpin turn and pulled up beside me. The passenger window rolled down. Mama poked her head out. "Abigail Andrea Whistler, I don't know whether to hug you or strangle you."

"I'm sorry, Mama," I sobbed. "But—"

She pushed open the door. "But we got us a dog to find, so I reckon I'll have to decide that later." She pulled me out of the snow and into the van. "You must've had wings to get this far in this snow."

"Or a bucket-load of determination," Meemaw said from the backseat.

And sitting right next to her was Cheyenne Rivers and Mr. Richard!

Mr. Richard smiled and touched the bill of his special driver cap. "Greetings, Miss Abby. Hope you don't mind, we hitched a ride with your folks."

I about burst with happiness and thankfulness to see them. "No, sir," was all I managed to get out.

None of us said another word as Daddy drove through the storm. Mama held me shivering against her warm body and wrapped a llama wool blanket around me. I tried not to lean too hard against the bump of her belly. I wasn't sure how I felt about a baby, but I didn't want to hurt whoever was in there.

Finally we pulled into the parking lot of the Craggy Gardens Visitor Center. There wasn't another car in sight. The Visitor Center was dark.

"Now what?" Cheyenne asked.

They all looked at me.

"We find him," I said.

"Lord, Lord," Mr. Richard said with a sigh.

I pushed open the door and stepped out.

And do you know what? In a blink, the sun came out, the snow tapered off, the wind settled. It was like someone flipped a switch.

"The best thing would be for us to fan out and start looking," Daddy said.

"No," Mama said. "We need to stick together. Someone could get lost." And just like that, standing there in ankle-deep snow, they were off and arguing again.

"What do you think, Abby?" Cheyenne asked.

My heart sank. Now that we were here, I had no blessed idea. I looked to Meemaw. She nodded and said, "Trust your instincts, child."

I closed my eyes and tried my level best to shut out the sound of Mama and Daddy arguing. I heard a crow call. I turned toward the sound. "This way," I said.

"I kept seeing Tam trapped in a tunnel when I dreamed the last few nights," I explained to Cheyenne as we followed the sound of the crow to a small meadow behind the center.

314

I looked around for any place Tam might be holed up in or trapped inside. There were a couple of picnic tables, a garbage can, and big rocks. At the far end of the meadow, rhododendron bushes grew tall, the tops of their snowy branches touching.

Just then, a big black crow sailed above my head, landing on the snow-covered branches. It raised its wings up and down and cawed.

All of a sudden it clicked. "A *tunnel*!" I said, grabbing Cheyenne's hand. "That crow is sitting on top of a tunnel!"

I cupped my hands around my mouth, filled my lungs with hope. "Tam! Come here, Tam!"

CHAPTER 48

Tam

A high, flutelike sound stirred Tam from the depths of his fevered sleep. He opened his eyes. He blinked in the light. The shadows just beyond stretched long across the melting snow. Slowly, he became aware: It was time. It was time for his girl.

But oh, he was so tired. He had tried so hard, watched for so long. He just wanted to return to that warm, safe place of deep sleep. He closed his eyes and lowered his head.

He heard it again, closer this time. His eyes flew open. Hope fluttered in his heart and took wing. He gathered his legs beneath him, stood, and swayed.

"Tam! Come here, Tam!"

Tam's great heart filled again with the sound of her voice. It sang through his soul like a long-remembered song, true as the needle of a compass.

He took one unsteady step, then two, toward the voice beyond the shadows.

CHAPTER 49

Abby

"Tam! Tam! Come here, Tam!" I called over and over until my voice broke. I closed my eyes. *Please, please,* I prayed.

I opened my eyes. The crow hopped in the snow toward the rhododendron tunnel. He turned his head and looked at me with his black eyes as if to say, *What are you waiting for?*

I called Tam's name again into the shadows at the opening of the rhododendron. It was hard to see in the dim light. I walked under the curved roof of branches, following that crow. Dead leaves and twigs snapped under my feet.

As my eyes adjusted to the shadows and light, I stopped.

Something moved at the far end. Something like a limping bundle of rags. A ray of sun lit the red and white coat.

I gasped. "Tam?"

The thing whimpered. It limped one, then two steps toward me, then stumbled.

"Tam!" I cried over and over. I ran to him, fell to my knees, and gathered him in my arms. He didn't weigh any more than a bundle of feathers. I could feel each and every rib through his dirty, matted coat. One of his eyes was purely a mess. But none of it mattered.

I carried him into the sunlit meadow. "I found him! He's alive!" I said to everyone as they grinned and stared at Tam in wonderment.

I held Tam close and just cried and cried. A warm tongue licked my cheek. Then Tam rested his head against my chest, and heaved the biggest sigh in the universe, like he was breathing out all the months and miles.

I kissed that special white spot on the top of his head. The snow on the ground glittered like a hundred million stars, and I had my own north star, finally, right here in my arms.

CHAPTER 50

Tam

Her smell surrounded him . . . grass, green apples, the salt of tears. Tears he licked from her face.

The months fell away. The mountains and high windy passes fell away. The rivers and streams, all the cold nights beneath the moon and stars, fell away. The hunger and fear and pain fell away.

All that mattered was this.

Tam listened to the steady *thump thump thump* of her heart. It filled him with hope and contentment. It healed him.

Tam wagged his tail. He looked into his girl's smiling eyes.

It did not matter to him all that he had endured. It had been time. Time to watch for his girl. And at long last she had come, and they were together again.

Finally, everything was as it should be.

ACKNOWLEDGMENTS

First, I'd like to send a million thanks to my wonderful agent, Alyssa Eisner-Henkin, who saw a gem in the diamond in the rough. Thanks for putting me and Tam and Abby on the path home.

I owe a bucket-load of gratitude to my early readers: Patti Sherlock, Emma Galvin, Julie Steppan, Susan Hamada, Linda Broussard, Charlene Brewster, and Lisa Actor. Thank you to the most talented Susan Patron for offering her time and encouragement when I was about to give up. I'm so lucky to have *the* best critique group in the world. Thank you to Lora, Jean, and Chris for your patience, support, and crucial feedback all along the way.

This book wouldn't be what it is without the thoughtful and respectful guidance from my dream editor, Molly O'Neill. I couldn't imagine a better north star to guide

Tam and Abby home. And many thanks to Katherine Tegen for opening her heart and her publishing imprint to my book. Every author needs a warm, safe place to create and grow their dream books. Katherine Tegen Books provided that home for me.

This story would never have been given to me without Barbara Edelberg, Jim Melton, and Sheltie Rescue of Utah. Not only did they bring sheltie love into my life, they've made finding forever homes for abandoned shelties their life and their passion.

Many thanks to my first cousin, Mica Copeland, for generously showing me all the sights Abby would see in Nashville and surrounding areas, and for sharing her Barbie dolls and all their outfits with me.

And special thanks and love to the real Miss Bettis, who supported me and believed in me even when I wanted to be a frog when I grew up.

Finally, I can never express all the many ways my husband, Todd, supports and encourages me in this sometimes lonely and frustrating process of writing. He keeps me anchored.